THE
FINDER'S
KEEPER

LEON KILDEA

First published in Australia by Aurora House
www.aurorahouse.com.au

This edition published 2025
Copyright © Leon Kildea 2025

Typesetting and e-book design: Amit Dey (amitdey2528@gmail.com)
Cover design: Donika Mishineva (artofdonika.com)

The right of Leon Kildea to be identified as the Author of the Word has
been asserted in accordance with the Copyright, Designs and Patents Act
1988.

ISBN NUMBER 978-1-923298-74-3 (paperback)

A catalogue record for this
book is available from the
National Library of Australia

DEDICATION

*To the next generation – in the hope they
may find that which is lost.*

ACKNOWLEDGEMENTS

Family; the 'One Particular Habour.'

The influential tales and poetic riddles of the Skalds, and other storytellers of those who have lived alongside the natural world.

The Pangerang people – the traditional custodians and first storytellers of the lands on which this story was written.

The skillful guidance cheerfully given by Linda at Aurora House and the contributions of her team. In particular, the story's editor, Anne, for her belief in the story and her work on improving its telling; Jieun, for her meticulous proofreading; Donika, for her evocative cover design; and the publishing expertise of Jes.

CONTENTS

PROLOGUE

I am troubled by the need to pass on this story. The story is about Edda, my grandmother, in her younger years. It is a story of hope. She came into the world at a time when hope was having a fling. Her birth was in the same year that Afghans saw the last of their Soviet invaders; the Singing Revolution was restoring independence to the Baltic States; naive optimism brought protestors to Tiananmen Square; the Berlin Wall was torn down; free elections were held in Poland; the Velvet Revolution in Prague ended four decades of one-party rule; and Romanians overthrew their long-standing dictator. Simmering beneath this precocious, blinkered hope for the future was a withering challenge that largely escaped attention. Meeting this challenge was not beyond our wit, but to this day, as then, efforts remain wilfully obstructed.

In an ordered, lacklustre life, I have allowed the years to creep by unnoticed. Now, I unexpectedly find myself in my twilight years. I must do as Edda once did – *tell her story before it is lost*. My telling will be a poor substitute for the prose and poems of the Skalds who recounted their tales when the events I will reveal were first set in motion. To tell you Edda's story of hope as it should be told, I must begin at a time long past, with people long forgotten.

PART 1

PAST

There is a pleasure in the pathless woods,
There is a rapture on the lonely shore,
There is society where none intrudes,
By the deep Sea, and music in its roar.
Roll on, thou deep and dark blue Ocean ... roll!

—George Gordon Byron

ONE

FIRST CONTACT

Northern Hålogaland, 868 CE

Repeated knocking on the hall's hefty wooden door was left unanswered.

Perhaps because little could be heard above the din within. One or two of the gathered villagers paused to cast an eye towards the source of the noise; others, immersed in their familiar banter, dismissed it as an unwelcome distraction. A slow and thunderous pounding echoed through the dim hall. It was impossible to ignore.

Those closest looked askance as the door was timidly opened. Glaring light from the late afternoon sun pierced then flooded the length of the room. There, dominating the doorway, the silhouette of a lone figure appeared, cut sharply by shards of sunlight. The figure was motionless but for his cloak, which was stirred to a flutter by an eddy of icy wind that coiled its way in through the open doorway. The murmur of the wind as it snuck in foretold of a gathering storm that would soon roar.

The ruckus in the hall dwindled until all that could be heard was a solitary, boisterous voice, which, belatedly realising something was afoot, stopped mid-sentence. The usually rowdy hall became oddly silent. Wooden beakers of ale were momentarily ignored as the gathering of drinkers squinted into the light. The stranger stooped through the doorway, abandoning the companionship of unsullied sea air in exchange for the musty smell of the hall's dank stone walls and thatched roof.

The sight of a stranger was unremarkable in this remote trading port. Tucked in the corner of a fjord, it had provided shelter from storms for countless mariners over the years. What was remarkable was this stranger's striking appearance – piercing, sea-green eyes framed by a tumble of hair that cascaded to rest on broad shoulders, which were draped with an iridescent green cloak slowly fluttering in the encroaching wind, like the shimmering folds of an aurora. If it were possible for a total stranger to be instantly captivating without uttering a word, this was such an occasion.

He then spoke. His voice projecting a calm clarity that commanded attention.

"I am short of crew. Does anyone here wish to join us on our voyage?" The silence in the hall held.

"We are hunters and farmers, not seafarers," a hesitant voice eventually confessed from somewhere in the dust-laden light, his utterance swiftly followed by the sound of mumbled agreement.

"I need only a simple oarsman, not a mariner."

"We are not *all* landlubbers," a man growled from across the hall as he slowly rose to draw himself up to his full height. His unkempt beard, long, matted hair and the wild look in his eye suggested he was someone not to be trifled with. "I welcome a fellow mariner here. Who are you, stranger, and from where have you come?"

"I am Harald Fairhair of Vestfold," the stranger replied. "And you, sir?"

"I am Ohthere from here on the Hålogaland coast. Come! Join me and my crew for a drink and tell me what has brought you so far from home."

As the stranger moved into the hall, he was followed by a cluster of men, perhaps two dozen in total, assumed by the flash of their intense sea-green eyes to be kinfolk. They were all summoned by Ohthere to what would become, for the night, the seafarers' table. As drinks were poured, an immediate camaraderie was formed, springing from the understanding that they were all of the sea – a fellowship of loyalty rooted in a pact between every mariner who risked all to cross an ocean, moored to the knowledge that salvation in dire distress would inevitably rely on a chance encounter with another seafarer. *One of their own.* But more than that, they were brothers united by the skills they possessed to navigate storms in a vast, oft-tormented wilderness that landlubbers could not begin to understand.

Quiet mutterings gently rose to a hum as the gathered villagers traded speculation about the green-eyed strangers and their intended voyage. Moments after downing their first drink, Harald and his crew yielded to prying questions.

"Harald Fairhair of Vestfold. You must be Halfdan's boy from the House of Yngling," Ohthere probed.

"Yes, the same," Harald agreed.

"Then you are the master of a ship famed for being, above all others, the most steadfast and true with graceful lines of curved oak."

"I won't dispute that. The Langskip is her name. She is moored just beyond, at the quay."

"Tell me," continued Ohthere, "is it truth or myth that you have an ancient, magical sled onboard that is fabled for bringing prosperity to those who possess it?"

"The petty kingdoms are full of stories. Do not be drawn in by all you hear," Harald replied, with a fixed stare that lent purpose to his voice. But it would take more than a stare to dissuade his questioner.

"Stories they may be, but I heard your crew call you Sleði-Gætir. Does that not mean the Sled-Keeper in your dialect? Is not your exquisite ship the home of Himinnsled, the famed mystical sled Odin used on his wanderings?"

"We will speak no more of this. I know of no place in all the kingdoms where people talk of such things," Harald said dismissively.

"I am Ohthere, the explorer of the North and South. I have heard stories of an ancient mystical sled from all corners of the known world."

"Well, sometimes stories are best left as stories."

But Harald's efforts at shutting down the conversation came too late. Attentive ears at nearby tables had been listening to every question, every answer, and busy lips were already spreading the word. On hearing of Himinnsled's promise of prosperity, a lone, shunned figure crouching in a shadowy corner felt his thoughts caught up in a silent frenzy. Eagerly snaking a path through the crowded hall, he made his way towards Harald.

"Looking for an oarsman, are you?" Grima asked hesitantly, keeping his eyes downcast.

Harald looked at the thin, truncated character nervously rocking from one broad flat foot to the other while repeatedly nodding and wringing his hands.

"Who are you?"

Grima, despite having contrived the meeting, continued to look to the ground rather than meet Harald's eye.

"My name? Grima, Grima Vansi. No one special. No one special at all, no, not at all."

"Well, no one else seems to be interested in joining us. Do you think you can pull an oar?"

"Yes, yes ... Grima can do that. Yes, he can."

"Very well, collect your things," Harald said. "We leave in the morning, as soon as the storm has passed."

Grima nodded eagerly, then, in a rarely witnessed gleeful mood, scurried away mumbling to himself.

"You can keep that one," Ohthere muttered to Harald as they watched the receding figure. "He's a whinging, greedy little worm. Take him on as crew if you wish. We are well rid of him."

"What has brought you to this harbour?" Harald asked, ignoring Ohthere's remark.

"We are coming home after exploring the far North, further than any known mariner has gone," Ohthere replied boastfully.

"And what did you find?"

"Mostly empty wilderness. There are only a few who are willing to endure the wastelands of the far North."

"So, there are some living there, some inhabitants?"

"As we sailed into an inlet and up the Great Dvina River beyond the far North, we found remote settlements of the Bjarmian people along the river, where valuable furs harvested over summer were being stockpiled."

"Stockpiled, you say. And are the furs still there?" Harald asked.

"As far as I know."

Harald looked to his crew who were all watching him with anticipation. Although they had been engaged in battles over the summer with neighbouring kingdoms, they had little in the way of plunder to show for it.

"It might be worth investigating," Harald said.

Ohthere slowly shook his head. "We retreated from the far North with the first signs of sea ice. It is late and dangerous for such a voyage."

"If we hasten, we might beat the worst of the winter," Harald insisted, amid nods of approval from his crew. They understood that with plundered furs to trade back in Vestfold, an otherwise bleak winter would be more comfortable for them and their families.

It is indeed worth investigating, Harald reflected, as the hall's inhabitants continued to drink their ale and the noise of boisterous voices became ever more unruly.

———————————————

Overnight, the anticipated storm arrived and moved on – or so it was thought. Not long after dawn, Harald watched as Grima Vansi appeared, trudging with clumsy gait along the quay carrying his kit. Standing alongside the Langskip, Grima took in the details of what would be for now his new home. Twenty paces long and four paces wide defined a slender hull that flared out at the beam, giving the Langskip better stability at sea.

Scanning the contents in the open hull, Grima noticed a ship's usual fittings, stays and oars as well as neatly stacked bundles of broad axes, swords and spears lashed to the deck, leaving no doubt that this was a warship. A noticeable gap in the rows of shields on her gunwales indicated to Grima his station as the new oarsman. Little else could be seen inside the sparse hull other than a large greasy-wool sail strung lengthways to double as a makeshift night shelter for the crew. Grima's eye finally rested on what he was looking for – a hidden object carefully disguised under a section of the sail at the base of the hull.

Conspicuous even to the now-distracted Grima was the Langskip's lines. Her oak hull planks were shaven thin enough to be fashioned into graceful sweeps along her length to elegantly erupt into a vertical sternpost and carved figurehead. Lightweight and fast, the boat presented as a perfect blend of form and function; exquisite art and efficient machine. She gave the impression of floating in the air over the water.

Clambering aboard, Grima Vansi cursed every fitting the toes of his flat feet stubbed on his way to the aftmost oar. There, he fixed his shield to join the row of others along the gunwale.

A comment by Ohthere to Harold the night before was at the time ignored, but now it troubled him. He recalled, *"He's a whinging, greedy little worm ... we are well rid of him."* Harald recognised on Grima Vansi's shield the flamboyant insignia of Fafnir the Dragon. Regarded by most as untrustworthy and ill-tempered, the Dragon cult worshipped gold or anything else of value that they could possess by any means. Like their idol, Fafnir, greed was their sole inspiration. Without wealth, they were intolerably resentful; with it, they were intolerably arrogant.

With all now on board, the Norsemen cast off to set a course for the far North and the Dvina River. By late morning, the crew were exhausted from hauling on their oars, making only a slow and tedious headway. Soon after noon, they were relieved to feel a breeze that quickly freshened to turn the oily sheen of the mirror-like sea into tiny ripples, which then stretched out to become long, white-capped waves. The crew sprang into action, shipping oars and hoisting sail with the speed and precision of circus performers, while Grima sat alone and silent, scowling.

"Not helping, no, not at all," he said to himself. "He said he needed only a simple oarsman, not a mariner." Then, with a snigger, he spat, "While they're distracted, Grima has other things he must do … yes, yes, he does."

Within minutes, the Langskip, now under full sail, was slipping through the waves with all those onboard cramming the weather side to keep it balanced and driven with good speed. At the helm, Harald steered the boat with the composure of a much more experienced mariner than one who had seen only eighteen winters. Despite his age, he already displayed the courage and wisdom needed to gain the respect of the gruff warriors who made up his crew – qualities that would one day serve him as a celebrated Viking king.

The wind's call rose to a howl as the storm grew in intensity. The waves, hearing the call, obeyed. Along the edge of each mounting crest, salty spray spewed into the air to be instantly whipped downwind. Streaks of ragged foam that appeared on the surface of the water were goaded by the wind till they were stretched beyond the crew's waning visibility. The boat's long shoal keel wallowed under the strain of the billowing sail as the rising seas formed tall, overhanging peaks. The Langskip's fearsome growling wolf figurehead rose high into the air before the vessel was deftly turned on the wave's slender crest to ease the hull down, preventing it from violently smacking onto the face of the wave. On each descent, the boat gathered pace as it punched through a collapsing wall of briny foam.

Reaching the trough, the Langskip slammed the wave in front. Her hull gave a reluctant shudder as the crew held fast to prevent themselves from tumbling into the maelstrom raging around them. Harald piloted the boat through the trough with enough speed to urge it up the next dark blue wall to a streaming spray at its crest. He again precisely finessed the tiller to avoid the Langskip's elegantly fashioned planks being shattered by the might of the storm.

Peering ahead in the failing light, Harald saw the jagged shapes of white-coloured flotsam. But it wasn't just the foam that had been billowing about in the water until now.

"Ice!" he shouted through the howl of the storm as he lent his weight to the tiller. The Langskip broached with a chance she would tumble and roll down the next foaming leviathan to sink into the silence beneath. Barely dodging the giant slabs of ice, Harald eased the boat back on course to surf down the wave. But when the Langskip lifted to the next crest, he was filled with dismay. As far as he could see was an ocean churning with broken, growling ice capable of ripping through the vessel's hull.

Handing the tiller to his best helmsman, Harald moved to the bow to call the course. Hours went by as the boat and its exhausted crew ran the angry gauntlet, until a cloud-filled night slowly crept over the Langskip. Deafening claps of thunder were at once joined by bolts of lightning shredding the night sky around them, each one causing Grima Vansi, in a funk of terror, to cover his eyes and let out a shrill, ear-piercing squeal.

With no safe haven along the coast, the crew was left with no choice but to run with the storm. Harald called changes to their course with only a moment's notice as ice loomed through the darkness with the helmsman responding to each call by heaving with all his might on the steer-board's tiller. The Langskip's timbers groaned in reply.

Harald turned his head briefly to listen through the shrieking chaos. There was something different, something disturbing in the boat's response. He knew the Langskip intimately – every stay, halyard and fitting. From somewhere, half buried beneath the howl of the wind in the rigging, he could hear a troubling sound. Not the usual creaking of timber or the dithering of a yet-to-be trimmed sail, or even the sound of a savage ocean barrelling along the hull.

A new noise was a concern. It signalled a new event, a new puzzle. And in a storm of this intensity, when the boat was at its limit, a puzzle was not welcome. Closing his eyes for a moment to concentrate, Harald realised with the next unfamiliar creak that what he was hearing was the sound of leather straining to breaking point.

"Ease on the helm!" he shouted in the direction of the stern.

At that moment, the leather lashings that attached the steer-board to the side of the boat snapped. The steer-board came adrift and was swept away to be lost into the ink below. The Langskip was now at the mercy of the storm. Moving with the agility of an elf, Harald was at the stern in a moment, an oar in one hand and his leather belt in the other. Lashing the oar to the sternpost he was able to regain some control, but in the towering, confused sea, with ice-laden waves colliding in every direction, it was apparent the situation was hopeless. The crew, desperate, looked to Harald for guidance.

All but one.

At a loss as to how the steer-board could have failed, Harald chanced a look over the starboard gunwale. What he saw gave rise to fleeting confusion that swiftly made way for a dark realisation.

The steer-board's tough walrus-hide lashings had seen the blade of a knife.

———————✥✥———————

Snöfrid, a young woman who had just completed her seventeenth year, had been born into an isolated clan unknown to the outside world. She was part of a line that reached back generations to a time when, being relentlessly hunted and fleeing brutal repression in the South, her ancestors with all their kith and kin were forced to continually move on as their oppressor's empire kept expanding to the far reaches of the known world. Generations came and went before Snöfrid's ancestors found and followed fertile land gifted by retreating ice sheets along the Scandinavian coast. After centuries of wandering and searching, the clan had found a place in the mysterious far North that could serve as a quiet, tranquil haven, a permanent home.

Situated in the hinterland of the White Sea in a deep U-shaped valley, long vacated by the glacier that had formed it, was a congregation of dwellings built by Snöfrid's forebears that was simply referred to as the Village.

The Village was tucked away in a nook cloaked by dips and folds in the valley's landscape. Even the few dwellings beyond the Village were concealed by the valley's many drumlins and giant boulders that were strewn across it.

The valley was bounded by precipitous cliffs that had been carved out by the same prehistoric glacier. The lofty cliffs' sheer ramparts disappeared into cloud as they soared high above the valley floor. Together they stood as a host of

silent sentinels enclosing the valley. The unknown inhabitants and their secretive dwellings would remain invisible unless, by nigh-impossible chance, lost explorers found
themselves standing among them. So unreachable was their
valley that the hermit society was compelled to teach its
children from a young age to commit to memory 'the way';
a clapping chant that children called out to remember the
exact sequence of twists and turns that allowed them to
pass through a vast maze. The maze itself was buried in the
gloomy depths of a morass of gigantic boulders that was the
glaciers' final dumping ground. For the villagers, it was the
most crucial sentinel of all. Unlike the cliffs that enclosed the
valley, this sentinel both allowed access to the valley by the
villagers and blockaded it from intrusion by outsiders with a
myriad of cul-de-sacs that obscured the solitary true passage
into the valley.

Snöfrid was starting the day as she did most days. But this
was not to be like any other day in her life. Walking to a hummock that overlooked the White Sea, she stopped to gaze out
over the half-frozen bay, then gasped. Standing perfectly still,
she took some time to absorb a creation so completely beyond
her understanding that she was captivated by both fear and
wonder. There, below her, were the elegant lines of a Viking
longship, partly sunken and stuck fast in the ice.

Snöfrid recoiled then buckled to sit on the ground, in
shock at what she saw next. There was movement; people
huddling onboard – people who did not, could not, belong
to the Village. Snöfrid began to move, then stood her ground
and looked again to check her doubting eyes before wildly
darting and weaving her way through the rocky maze that
guarded the entrance to her valley. Racing to the cabin that
was her family's home, she saw Kalev, her father.

"Papa, come see, you must come!" Snöfrid shrieked.

"What is wrong, girl?" Kalev replied. "What has happened?"

"People have come here, strangers. Outsiders are here!"

"Impossible. Did you see them? Why has a lookout not sounded the alarm?" He asked, as he frantically snatched his jacket from its hook.

"They have come from the sea, not the land. They are at the bay. There are outsiders at the bay. Come quickly."

Kalev did not entertain her plea. As he ran out the door and headed straight to the Village Square, Snöfrid knew what he was about to do and hastily followed. At the Square, Kalev picked up a long steel staff attached by a chain to a large triangle, also made from steel. The triangle had lain dormant in the Village Square since it was built. It had only one purpose. It was there to warn the villagers of approaching outsiders, but it had never been used. The frenzied clanking of the triangle resounded through the Village, bringing people, young and old, scampering out of their dwellings to the square.

"What's going on?" one of them asked the moment Kalev ended the alarm.

"Talk to Snöfrid."

As Snöfrid described what she had seen, the villagers immediately made plans to gather their rescue team together. The team assembled promptly with ropes, grappling hooks, blankets and a sledge to transport the injured, and headed to a raft that was kept on the shoreline. This was not the first time they had dealt with an emergency, and they were practised in quickly organising aid to anyone needing help. It was, however, the first time they would be rescuing outsiders.

The spent seafarers were gratefully rescued by the villagers – all but their leader who could not be found. Harald had chased Himinnsled as it disappeared through a breach in the Langskip's hull. Diving into the deep, he had managed to grab the sled, then fought his way to the surface and struggled through wild, ice-laden waters to drag it ashore. Lying on the shore, exhausted and suffering from acute exposure, he continued to clutch the sled with the kind of resolute grip that would endure beyond his own survival.

Then, through the fog of his fatigue, Harald heard the sound of someone approaching and noticed a shadow fall nearby. In a snarling voice, the figure spoke.

"Sled-Keeper, are you? No, I think not. You be a Sled-Keeper no more ... no, no more."

Harald felt the vicious blows of a rock pounding his head as he lay on the shore but was more aware of the urgent tug-of-war that had begun over the sled. It was a struggle Harald's freezing, battered body was bound to lose had not the hopeful thief skulked away at the first sight of the villagers approaching. As they bent over him, in his half-conscious state, Harald was murmuring over and over, *"None shall have the sled. None but those it belongs to."* Although they didn't know it then, in time these words would become a creed reaffirmed as a chant whenever the secluded clan's sagas were retold.

Carefully, they lifted the gravely ill Harald from the shore to place him on the sledge and made their way back to the Village and Kalev's house, where the task of tending to him was welcomed by young Snöfrid. As Snöfrid covered him with every reindeer skin at hand to combat his hypothermia, he continued his mantra: *"None shall have the sled. None but those it belongs to."* Snöfrid noticed his speech was slurred, and, more worryingly, he stopped shivering uncontrollably and began to slip in and out of consciousness.

Snöfrid had seen this before and knew that without drastic action Harald would soon be beyond recovery. Quickly, she removed her outer clothing and crept under his coverings to lend him her body heat. As she lay holding him in a gentle embrace, she listened to his heart and watched the almost imperceptible rise and fall of his chest. Several hours passed before she heard Harald's heartbeat start to grow stronger and his shallow breathing deepen. Overcome with relief and gratitude that his looming death had been averted, Snöfrid released a quiet sob, stirring the still half-conscious Harald to sluggishly drape his arms over her.

It took over a week of rest, warmth and nourishment before he made a recovery, but eventually Snöfrid's tender care was rewarded. Harald pulled back from the brink. During the time of Harald's recovery, a steady stream of villager's made their way to Snöfrid's hummock to view the wreck of the Langskip. While they were fascinated with the ship, the biggest talking point amongst them was the crew's store of weapons that could be seen neatly stacked and lashed to the deck. This prompted a meeting back in the Village where it was decided that the seafarers' weapons must never leave their ship – so it is there that they would remain.

The rescue was the beginning of an enduring friendship, both between Harald and Snöfrid and between the seafarers and the hermit villagers. The thankful Langskip crew – the first outsiders to ever visit the hidden settlement – never left; and while Harald's recovery was complete, Snöfrid's vigil was not. Harald and Snöfrid became inseparable, with one rarely seen about the Village without the other.

Harald adopted Snöfrid's habit of walking to her favourite place, the hummock overlooking the White Sea. There, on each visit, they witnessed the slow demise of the Langskip. Already the press of winter ice had crushed parts of her hull, bringing down the mast. Harald and Snöfrid would spend hours sitting at the hummock talking about each other's lives. Harald spoke of conflicts and victories over neighbouring clans, and battles with people in far-off lands across the sea. For her part, as the villagers also did with the rest of the crew at night around communal fires, Snöfrid told of her ancestors' escape from brutal persecution in the South countless generations ago and their search to find a place of precious peace and isolation in which to settle. She spoke of stories from her clan's sagas – legends that both explained and reinforced the traditions that had been handed down from times long past. Traditions that they had developed over time, or, in many instances, adapted from various other communities they encountered over the centuries of wandering in their search for a new home.

She went on to describe her clan's solitude here in a harsh environment that further moulded and refined their culture and beliefs. She spoke of the years that came and went when the rustic wooden racks that stood outside each dwelling were bare, no longer emitting the pungent smell of stockfish drying in the cold, parched air. Years when winter storms were so severe, so persistent, that venturing out to hunt could not be endured for long. Years when the gift of migrating reindeer bypassed their locality and food stocks were perilously depleted. When famine visited and hunting forays needed to extend to long journeys inland, where the Village's hunters had glimpsed then quietly avoided others on desperate hunting missions from their own remote communities.

"The unwillingness of our hunters to engage with other hunters from beyond the Village was more than a desire for us to remain isolated and unseen," Snöfrid said. "It was even more than our desire to preserve the deep secret of the way through the intricate rocky maze that safeguards our hidden valley. Our ancestors knew when they arrived here seeking a place of quiet refuge that others were already here. We understood that they had already formed a connection with the land, rendering it theirs, not ours. They must have known we had arrived because there were times, especially in those early days, when our hunters were away ranging through forests and mountains for most of the summer trying to find food. It seemed that an unspoken pact had gradually emerged. An understanding that if we did not interfere with their traditions, their land, if we kept to ourselves and did not seek to expand or plunder, they would accept us and respect our isolation. Although we quietly avoid each other, we are allies in that pact and so we call them the Etera, which means 'partners' in the Rasna tongue we brought with us from the South. We and the Etera remain as partners in a pact of complete isolation from each other."

Snöfrid went on to explain that, with the strict adherence to this pact of isolation, there was no real prospect of trade to see the Village through the most difficult of times.

"The wisdom of our sagas, developed over many generations since our arrival, told of one constant that would be our people's salvation in difficult times – a salvation delivered by a concern for each other in the Village that extended to unstinting generosity in sharing any meagre provisions that could be gleaned," she said. "The sagas' lesson of generosity rendered survival in the worst of times and was cause for celebration in good times."

Harald's seafarers listened and learned from the villagers' tales. In turn, they were invited to speak of their voyage and the wreck of the Langskip; a story that would take its place among the sagas as they and the hermit villagers slowly melded into one clan. This emerging new clan would adopt the name Stórmenska, the word used by the seafarers to describe the villagers. In their Norse tongue it meant the generous ones. While learning from each other's cultures, the seafarers soon forgot the Gods of Ásgard. Constrained by their human hide and hubris, their Gods' meddling deeds were a poor match with the seafarers' new life and the common-sense wisdom of the nature-spirit Gods of their hosts.

This merging of cultures included a blending of the ancient Rasna tongue of the hermit villagers with the Norse spoken by the seafarers, resulting in the fashioning of a new language. Staying true to the lessons of the sagas, the emerging Stórmenska language continued the villagers' tradition of having only one word to describe 'I' and 'we' and one word only for 'me' and 'us'. The seafarers' days of raiding were consigned to stories of a cruel past.

------◆·······➤◉➤·······◆------

One still, misty morning after walking to their hummock, Harald and Snöfrid's conversation stumbled into a subject both had been avoiding.

"But the others have decided to stay," Snöfrid said. "They don't want to go back to their land, their life of squabbling and fighting. Why do you want to leave? Here it is peaceful. Here we support each other, not fight each other. Here is where you should be."

"My home in Vestfold is where I must be. I hope you will come to understand. I must return to my family."

"We can be your family."

"I am the son of a chieftain. My family is my destiny. It's not that I want to go. I *must* go. Come with me, Snöfrid. Come to my land and there we can make a life together."

"A land where fighting is ingrained in the life we would have. Why?"

"I will shield you from the fighting. I will keep you safe."

"Not *why should I go with you*. Why are you always fighting? Every story you have told me is about violent clashes with others or among yourselves. Why? Why must you fight?"

"We are not always fighting. But you're right. We fight when we must. We fight for land, power, wealth and, most importantly, for our security."

"You would be more secure if you all lived as we do," Snöfrid said. "You, your neighbours near and far, all seem to be fighting because you want more than what you have. Will that ever end? Our sagas tell the parable of the lone wolf who would not hunt with others because he was too greedy to share his prey. As a lone predator, he failed to get enough to eat and was slowly starving. In desperation, he ran with other wolves. The pack worked as a team in stalking and sharing their prey. By overcoming his selfishness, by cooperating and sharing, he never went hungry again. It is the acceptance of the wolves of an outsider that has inspired us to accept you and your crew, trusting that you will also live and work with us as a team."

"Your sagas and our legends are not all that different," Harold said. "I know that in your culture the wolf is an important totem, a symbol of living in harmony with nature, and for us the wolf is a symbol of our duty to care for our families and each other. Perhaps our two worlds are not that far apart."

"Perhaps," Snöfrid said unconvincingly. She continued, "But do not think we are naive. We know some will persist in clutching onto greed rather than share their good fortune – even when, like the hungry wolf, it is to their own detriment. They dismiss as out-dated the lessons from the wilderness. Telling and retelling our sagas reminds us of why we escaped the South and what we have learnt over the centuries since. Lessons that were sometimes learnt at great cost."

"Since being here, I have given much thought to the way your villagers live," Harald replied. "I have even dared to think the day will come when my people will all be united under one banner, when we all see ourselves as one clan, when we can start learning to live as you live."

"In that case, you should leave here. And that is what you should do. Unite your people to bring an end to their futile attacks on each other."

"I will swear an oath to your Spirits and my Gods. It is what I will do, what I will dedicate my life to. But I want – need – you to come with me. To guide me as my wife."

"To live with your people? Even your crew, who are adopting our ways, are still prone to squabbles and fights among themselves. No, I will not come with you and be a part of that."

An uncomfortable silence followed, during which Snöfrid felt she should have shown more restraint.

"Harald," she began gently. "This is the only life I know. If I leave, I can never come back, never visit my family, never again walk along the deserted shores of the White Sea or roam through untouched forests. Never again live in our land of peace, a land that teaches us who we are and how we should live."

"Why? You can come back to visit, surely?"

"The Village, our people, are invisible to the world. We have made it so and wish it to be forever thus. We have all agreed on a pact that there is no place for the comings and goings of others, for exposing ourselves to a pitiless world, for allowing greed as a way of thinking to be smuggled in. Not even by a visitor who was born here. It is an accepted pact amongst us; one that we were all taught in our childhood. If I were to go with you, I would be forever trading a life of compassion for one of violence borne of greed."

"A better understanding of your world is what I need to bring peace to my land. I need you by my side to help fulfil my destiny, a destiny forged by you here in the wilderness."

"If that is truly your mission and you believe I can be a part of making it possible, it would be selfish of me if I did not come with you to help where I can; but I will not be your partner. I will not marry you and become one of your people until they are united and your quest for peace among them is won."

And so it was that at the end of that eventful winter, a time framed by astonished villagers rescuing then adopting similarly astonished seafarers, the thaw commenced. It was time for Harald and Snöfrid to begin their long journey overland to Harald's home in Vestfold. For days that lead up to her departure, Snöfrid was rarely dry-eyed as she nervously packed and repacked her few belongings, visited and revisited friends and incessantly hugged her parents.

Snöfrid and Harald walked to their favourite place overlooking the White Sea one last time. Neither spoke. A moment of contemplation morphed into an extended silence. At last, Snöfrid sighed decisively and stood to walk back. They took one final look out over the White Sea and then, moments after they turned their backs, the Langskip surrendered to the spring thaw and slipped into the deep to complete her final voyage.

TWO

THE SOUTH

The villagers were preparing for a ceremonial farewell. Among all the preparations for Harold and Snöfrid's long journey to Vestfold, a send-off for one of their own in the Village had not been staged before. While the seafarers were the first to visit, Snöfrid would be the first to leave for a new life, never to return. The farewell was an occasion that required great festivity but was not without some concern at the loss of one of their own to the outside world. Even more worrying to many was a generous offer being considered by the Village. Harald had asked for approval to summon the partners and children of the seafarers and bid them to journey north to live in the hermit village. Like Snöfrid's departure, this had never been done before.

A spirited discussion resulted concerning the risk that adopting more outsiders might pose to their way of life. The Village Seer, a revered soothsayer from a long line of Shaman, reminded all those gathered that generosity had served them well over the centuries.

"Be careful not to judge the newcomers before they arrive, before you know them," he advised.

Taking the Seer's lead, Harald added, "Your generosity in reuniting the seafarers with their loved ones may benefit all. If the families are not invited, the seafarers here may feel obliged to leave and will perhaps one day reveal enough news of the Village and its whereabouts for you to lose your treasured isolation." Thus, it was agreed that once again the wisdom of generosity should prevail. On his return to the South, Harald would invite the partners and children of the seafarers to journey to the far North to be met by the Seer.

As a part of the farewell ceremony, the Village gave Harald and Snöfrid a prized traditional knife. For generations it had been in the keeping of the resident Seer. The gift came with a caution that it must never be used in anger. As with every knife in the Village, it was a tool, not a weapon.

Thanking the Seer, Harald added, "My dream, my newfound purpose, is to bring about a new era for my people. A time when they will build, not destroy, when they will lay down their weapons and use only tools."

In keeping with the tradition of offering a gift in return, Harald presented to the Seer a gold ring adorned with the motif of a head of a growling wolf that had once been given to him by a Vestfold shield-maiden. She had insisted that the ring, known as Andvaranaut, had magical powers that could not be used by the corrupt and dishonest, as the ring held a curse for them. Only people with good hearts driven by compassion could benefit from its power. In giving it, Harald knew that the ring, to be handed down in the keeping of successive Seers, had found its home.

Harald spoke of the concern many of the villagers harboured about accepting more outsiders and the vulnerability of the Village's culture of kindness. With this in mind, he said, "There is a way to strengthen your culture of generosity, especially with the seafarers and their families. My family's most prized possession, Himinnsled, will not be returning south with me to Vestfold." He then presented the sled to the Seer. In so doing, he spoke of the night he and his crew were rescued, of the struggle he had had with a thief, and his decree that none should have the sled but those it belonged to.

"It is all of you," Harald announced solemnly, "you collection of villagers and seafarers, you Stórmenska, who are now those the sled belongs to." Speaking to his crew, he added, "It is no longer just to remind you seafarers of your roots. Over many generations, the villagers here have learnt the wisdom of kindness, the same spirit that was displayed in rescuing us and now reuniting you with your families. It is that spirit that you seafarers now have a duty to embrace. The sled is a gift to all of you, of a most sacred icon, a physical reminder that you all should forever be driven by a concern for each other. If the villagers' spirit of generosity, now the spirit of Himinnsled, is embraced by all, the sled will forever make good its promise of prosperity."

History would prove Harold right. The gift of the sled would become an icon that would forever remind the Stórmenska of the wisdom of their generosity.

Harald and Snöfrid's thousand-mile journey overland to Vestfold took months to complete. By the end of the first week of trekking, they had fallen into a rhythm of walking and resting during daylight hours, thankful for the cheer afforded by a meagre sun on their faces. At times, their progress was interrupted by the need to hunt when a mountain hare or other game was spotted.

By the eighth day, there was no sun to lift their spirits. Harald routinely glanced over his shoulder to check the progress of darker clouds rolling in from the north. Anxiously scouring their surroundings for shelter, they could find none. A boisterous wind whipped up spindrifts of dry snow as storm clouds overtook them. Once the snow cover wildly spiralling around them had been lost into the air, the wind scoured small flakes of ice, whipping them up to blast their faces. Covering up as best they could, they pressed on, squinting through the storm.

"Over here!" Snöfrid shouted, as she spotted a large boulder. Huddling down in the shelter of a deep trough in the snow on the lee of the boulder, they braced themselves for what was to come. As the storm grew in intensity, gusts of wind blasted around the rock as a raging vortex etching the remaining snow away from their hollow to leave them exposed. It was not a passing storm. As their huddle dissolved into an embrace, Harald and Snöfrid succumbed to the cold and its induced fatigue, their slumber slowly morphed into a perilous deep sleep. The initial blasts of wind that had heralded the storm front moved on to allow a shadowing snowfall to gently cover them as they slept.

⚊⚊⚊✦✦⚊⚊⚊

Juvven and his wife, Lejá, had left their three children behind in the safety of their lavvu to hunt in the wake of the storm. Shuffling to push their skis through the recent fall of deep powder snow, they scanned their surrounding for fresh animal tracks. Lejá stopped.

"Is that what I think it is?" she asked, pointing to a boulder. Juvven looked across to what appeared to be the hem of a vivid green cloak protruding from the snow. As Juvven scooped snow away, Lejá examined the two bodies lying beneath.

"They're dead," Juvven said. "They must be."

"Shh!" Lejá had her ear to the couple's faces to listen for any sign of life. "Not quite. I can hear faint breathing. They won't last much longer, though. Juvven, your feet will be frozen to the ground if you stand still much longer. Have you not seen a stranger before? Give me your Luhkka and fetch the reindeer and sleigh." Juvven dutifully pulled his hooded cape over his head and laid it with Lejá's over the two trekkers.

"Where am I?" Harald asked, alarmed, as he abruptly woke and looked around the inside of a large tent.

"You're safe," Lejá said.

"Snöfrid?" Harald called out urgently.

"I'm right here!"

Snöfrid was awake and alert, sipping on a wooden mug of warm reindeer milk. Harald was handed the same. As he was about to take his first sip, he paused.

"How did we get here?"

"That matters little," Juvven replied. "You must stay with us until you regain your strength."

"We must continue our journey to the South," Harald said, as he made an ill-fated attempt to stand.

"If you are going to the South, you will need all the strength you can muster," Lejá chuckled. "After all, we know that dealing with people from the South can take some effort."

"Yes, stay here with us for as long as you wish, to recover. You are our guests," Juvven went on. "But I am curious about where you came from, how you got caught here in a storm."

"We are just passing through," Harald responded.

"From where? We are many clans from across the vast North, and you belong to none of them," Juvven said. "Your clothes, and that knife you carry, are not from any in our world. Are there people unknown to us in the North?"

"Shipwrecked," Snöfrid cut in hastily – perhaps a little too hastily. She was keen to dispel any hint of her people's existence and their hidden valley. "We were shipwrecked and are trying to get home."

"Very well, whatever you say," Juvven said shrugging his shoulders. "It's really none of our business anyway. For now, you best drink up and get some rest."

———— ✖✖ ————

It was over a week before Harald and Snöfrid announced they were ready to continue their journey. Their stay was longer than was needed for their recovery, but too short for an emerging close friendship to be fully realised. Comfort was the reason they lingered. Not the comfort of shelter in their hosts' lavvu; nor the comfort of not having to hunt for every scrap of food. Rather, they found enticing comfort in the company of their newly acquired friends.

The whole family seemed to have no expression beyond a ready smile that came from a deep pool of affection for humanity. Even when Juvven and Lejá had reason to chide each other, it was framed as a humorous dig. Their kind-hearted spirit was infectious. Never a squabble, cry or harsh word was heard from their children.

"I will miss them dearly," Harald confided in Snöfrid as they prepared to leave. "They are such an agreeable family."

"They seem to have few possessions and no permanent home," Snöfrid replied. "I've never met such people. So happy and comfortable within themselves."

"This is for you," Lejá said in a matter-of-fact way as she entered the lavvu to lay a parcel on the ground. "We will miss you."

"What is it?" Harald asked.

"Food, mainly dried meat. You will travel faster if you don't have to hunt for food so often."

"And this should get you home a lot faster," Juvven said, as he presented them with two pairs of skis. Harald and Snöfrid's objections tumbled over each other.

"Too generous?" Lejá said, "No, not generous at all. Juvven has been looking for an excuse to make us each a new pair of skis. Isn't that right, Juvven?"

"Yes, Lejá, you're absolutely right," Juvven said flippantly with a wry smile. "Who would have thought the day would come when you're right? We should thank our new friends for giving us a use for those old skis and an excuse to fashion new ones."

"Not just thank them … here, take this," Lejá said, as she handed Snöfrid a small leather bag full of coins.

"No, I cannot accept this. You have already been too kind."

"Snöfrid, you don't understand," Lejá interrupted. "We were given these coins by a trapper from the South in exchange for a reindeer. We have no use for them. No one here uses coins. They're just useless trinkets, dead weight that we cart around. We already have more in our life than we need. Taking them is really doing us a favour. You are bound to find some use for them in the South. I've heard people there love to get their hands on coins."

Snöfrid felt tears pricking her eyes as she and Harald bade farewell to their kind hosts and set off again into the snowy wilderness – this time, their journey easier as they loped along on their skis.

⚊⚊⚊≈•≈⚊⚊⚊

With the far North behind them, Harald and Snöfrid found that the further south they travelled, the more they came into contact with fur trappers and fellow travellers until they reached the first of many settlements in the petty kingdoms that crossed their path. Unlike the start of their trek, here as they passed through villages, they were treated with suspicion, and, on increasingly frequent occasions, outright contempt.

Reaching a small Hordafylke village nestled in the Valley of the Seven Mountains, they were warned by a fisherman of skirmishes between the local clan and Harald's own Vestfold people, a hangover from the previous year's fighting that involved Harald and his crew. A squabble flared up when Harald's shimmering green cloak was recognised by a Horda guardsman, ending with the guardsman's violent death. The lessons of humanity Harald had learnt during his time back in the Village were deserting him, and the Seer's gift of the traditional knife – one that must never be used in anger – was no longer a tool but a blood-stained weapon.

To evade the Horda mob now hunting them, Harald and Snöfrid climbed high into the mountains to ski across the remote Hardangervidda plateau. Their traverse of this plateau, an ice and snow desert of howling blizzards, became a desperate struggle that all but ended their days. By the time grim determination delivered the beleaguered two to Vestfold, the warrior in Harald had re-emerged. His sworn aim of uniting the petty kingdoms under one banner would not be done gently. On his return, Harald visited each of the seafarers' families to explain that their partners and fathers were waiting for them in a new world in the North. The Stórmenska's Seer in the Village ensured that the seafarers' partners and children who travelled north were welcomed with tolerance and generosity; not as outsiders but as Stórmenska, their own. Snöfrid's arrival in the South as an outsider was starkly different, where many regarded her as a wicked sorceress. She needed no reminder that her chosen path, a ground-breaking departure from the Village, was well and truly at a cost beyond her reckoning.

⁂

Harald's parting gifts in the far North, the sled and the ring, would prevail as Stórmenska icons through the ensuing centuries, symbols of the beginning of new friendships, the birth of a new civilisation. Unified by the spirit of the sled, the adopted icon of generosity, all in the far North who called themselves Stórmenska celebrated the value of giving … Well, almost all.

The sled's endowment of generosity gave the Stórmenska an unwavering bond, a bedrock of fellowship from which they could not help but survive and thrive. Even if confronted by self-seeking behaviour, their response would be kindness, as called for by the spirit of the sled. Along with the gift of Himinnsled to each succeeding Seer came the title of Sleði-Gætir with a pledge to keep the sled protected for future generations.

The Stórmenska sagas of the North, including stories of the wreck of the Langskip and Fairhair's gifts, had been faithfully told and retold over many centuries, but of late their cherished isolation was no longer assured. The clan's characteristic generosity, even in the face of self-indulgence, was extended to increasing encounters on hunting trips, with the Sunnan arriving from large, crowded settlements in the South. Despite greeting the Sunnan as friends, the Stórmenska had increasingly been harassed whenever they came into contact. Bewilderingly, some were even jailed for crimes against the South's religious laws. With all but one family, who revered the Sunnan, the Stórmenska were increasingly seeing persecution or worse simply for following their own ways of living.

Down-to-earth and astute, the Stórmenska were aware they needed to keep their sacred bond with the forest to survive. They knew the Sunnan's man-God, like their abandoned Viking Gods of old, would be a barricade to the natural world, diminishing the guardianship and the restraint that had sustained them in the wilderness for centuries. Bemused by the Sunnan's conceit in believing they were made in their God's image, the Stórmenska could not fathom the array of self-serving utterances that radiated from that belief. They were at a loss to know how they or their lives would be better off for engaging in such rigid thinking. Easier to grasp was the Sunnan God's instruction to followers to increase in number, to fill the earth and to subdue it. This they were beginning to understand through bitter experience.

After centuries of witnessing the abundant rewards that joint effort and generosity bestowed, the Stórmenska struggled with a religion whose followers often embraced greed over compassion.

But the Sunnan's growing hostility was not just a response to their man-God being shunned. Stórmenska country contained rich grazing and fishing grounds that had become the object of Sunnan greed. Most troubling, the Stórmenska's Sled-Keeper, Harkon the Loud, foretold of the Mann-fell – a time when people from the South would pounce on the Stórmenska like hungry wolves, a time when those who were enslaved by them would suffer the loss of their language and culture. According to the Seer's prophecy, some Stórmenska would descend into the depths of hopelessness, either to be ruined by the South people's strong drink or simply die of despair. It was a warning. Whether the Mann-fell would truly come to pass, however, was not able to be seen.

⚬ ⚬

The sight of drifting smoke emerging through cloud was the first sign of strife. Gefandi and his band of hunters skied from the mountains back to the Village as fast as their powerful legs would allow. They were too late. The Village was gone … pillaged and burnt. So swiftly had the prophecy of the Mann-fell come upon them.

The walls that remained of Gefandi's home surrounded only smouldering beams, remnants of a roof that had given shelter for generations. Frantic searching yielded only anguish. Some villagers could not be found. Those who were located were lying lifeless among the burning remains of their homes or scattered across the snow, hunted down as they fled. No sign of life was left in the Village.

Gefandi, kneeling next to the body of his beloved wife, Gudrun, was silent, inconsolable, adrift, until a sound – the only sound in that bleak desolation – found its way through a wall of grief. It was the unmistakeable sound of life, the cry of a baby coming from somewhere among the ruins. Gefandi found some comfort in the discovery of Havardr, Harkon the Loud's infant son, along with his older sister, Tua, who had hidden him.

As night fell, the full extent of the destruction became clear. A mustering revealed the entire clan had been massacred or enslaved except for Gefandi's band of hunters and those who had been away fishing and gathering wood when the Sunnan attacked. The Sled-Keeper himself, Harkon the Loud, was missing, so his children, Tua and Havardr, were adopted by parents grieving for their own.

As if the torment of their number being reduced to a few score was not enough, one final devastation would grip the Stórmenska. The very lifeblood of their culture, the symbol of their generosity and their origin, Himinnsled, was gone.

It could only have been one of their own who divulged to the Sunnan 'the way', the mystery of the maze that guarded the Village and the revered location of Himinnsled within, and with this realisation, the survivors were plunged into a disturbing silence. Already numb with grief, they were too crushed to weep. The Sunnan's massacre of the Stórmenska and the theft of Himinnsled may have succeeded in destroying that age-old civilisation. Gefandi knew the Sunnan would be back. Greed would demand it. He now understood that compassion and kindness were no shield from the unconstrained insanity of this kind of slaughter.

There was only one path to take. Abandoning the smouldering remains of their beloved settlement, the survivors, dreading the world beyond their valley, made their way through the rocky maze for the last time. As they emerged, they stopped at the sight of a large group of their mysterious, silent neighbours, the Etera, lining a ridge in the distance. The Etera had seen the smoke from the Sunnan raid and guessed the valley would be abandoned. The Etera's leader approach Gefandi with a small herd of reindeer as a gift to help them on their way. The Etera must have wondered if they would be the next target of the Sunnan. The Stórmenska then left to become secretive wanderers in the wilderness. They had forsaken their home but not their beliefs, and clung to the hope that one day, reunited with their sacred sled, they would be able to return to their homeland and rebuild.

In time, Gefandi and his troupe of nomadic herders and hunters learnt the fate of the sled and the Sled-Keeper. Stáli, an enslaved Stórmenska, had escaped the Sunnan to join up with Gefandi's wandering clan. Gefandi listened as he told how Himinnsled had been taken to the South to be sold. He knew nothing of its whereabouts. As for Harkon the Loud, Stáli described how he was forced to witnessed Harkon being set upon by pious Christians when they found out he was the Stórmenska's Seer, a heretic. As a mockery to his title, they stabbed him in one eye and laughed loudly about him now being no longer a Seer but a half-Seer.

"When I saw Harkon for the last time, his wound was so severe that one eye was completely missing," Stáli said. He went on to say, "Harkon was shattered at the loss of Himinnsled. He saw it as a shameful failure as a Sleði-Gætir, after centuries of Sled Keepers who had passed it on. He swore an oath that he would not rest until the last of the people responsible for its theft had left the face of the earth."

"Why did they take out his eye?" Gefandi asked.

"In their ignorance, they did not know that a Seer's visions are not through their eyes," Stáli said. "There was raucous laughter again when they learnt that the Stórmenska believed him to be a shapeshifter – one who could take the form of a bird and fly to faraway places. He was locked in a prison. As you know, that is a prospective death sentence for any Stórmenska."

"The next morning, he could not be found."

THREE

THE WHITE REINDEER

Norway, the North, Christmas 1888 CE

A forest of antlers abruptly appeared in the brittle moonlight as the startled herd lifted their heads as one to look towards a nearby tent.

From inside the tent, the beating of a drum reverberated. Realising it was a familiar sound, the reindeer soon returned to their endless task of foraging for lichen and moss beneath the snow, as the moonlight imprisoned in their steamy breath tumbled across the frozen ground.

Inside the tent, Bodin was performing a ritual known only to Seers of an earlier time. He was considerably older and, most would agree, wiser than any of his companions. Descended from a long line of Seers – his father having been Havardr and his grandfather Harkon the Loud – Bodin was currently revered as the last Seer. With his passing, many of his people's mystical traditions would be lost.

Despite his status, Bodin was a humble man who wore simple, unadorned reindeer-hide garments. His kindly appearance and wiry build gave the impression of a younger man, an illusion betrayed only by his battered, coarse-skinned hands that emphasised the glint from a polished gold ring. The piercing sea-green eyes that blazed from his weathered face was shared by many in his clan.

The shadows of four reindeer herders danced menacingly on the walls of the tent as the flames from a small fire flickered. Among them sat a stranger, a boy. Spellbound by the pounding of the Seer's drum, his eyes grew wide with wonder.

The boy's skin was smooth and pale, unlike the windswept features of the others. He wore neither reindeer hide nor the herders' best clothes adorned by coloured beadwork. Knitted mittens and hat, knickerbockers of plain wool and an anorak of finely woven cotton left no doubt that he was out of place. Any similarity the boy bore to the herders around him was confined to the colour of his eyes.

From the stories told by his grandmother, the boy had concluded the herders from the North must be Sámi, an impression reinforced by the Seer and his mystical drum. He would learn he was mistaken.

The herders had discovered the boy during the long twilight and brought him back to their camp. It was a most unlikely meeting. The band of nomads rarely journeyed far with their herd at this time of the year. If it were not for them searching for a small group of their reindeer that had strayed, there would have been no one in that wilderness to rescue the boy. He would almost certainly have perished from the bitter cold during the hours of darkness.

The boy's name was Olaf. Although only twelve years of age, he was tall and strong and already a skilful skier. He had set out on his new pair of skis from his parents' feriehus, a sturdy wooden holiday cabin in the forest that had once been the family home of his great-grandmother.

Olaf and his twin sister, Hedda, were on the usual family holiday they undertook each Christmas in the north. From their earliest memories, the twins had been close, caring siblings who spent much of their spare time in each other's company, particularly when holidaying here at their cabin when the winter weather was uninviting. Both were often chided by their parents for daydreaming. On occasions when Olaf was left alone in his own company, he would lose himself pondering or pursuing his passions for sketching and poetry. When the weather allowed, he often explored the nearby forest on skis.

Earlier that day, Olaf had again been lost in thought. He had ventured out alone, not intended to roam far and was usually careful not to lose his bearings when he skied into a forest. He was looking for long, untracked slopes to ski, where he would link graceful turns by kneeling with each knee, one after another, to weave his way between trees. It was his favourite thing to do and the closest thing he could imagine to the exhilaration of being able to fly.

His elation at the end of a seamless ski run in fresh, dry snow had been interrupted by the sight of a magnificent white reindeer. Olaf decided to have a closer look, but each time he got close to the reindeer, it slowly moved away, and each time, Olaf felt compelled to follow.

He was taken by surprise when he realised it was late. The feriehus and his ski slope had been left far behind, and the sun hovering low over the high-latitude horizon reminded him that he should be indoors. Looking around, Olaf could not see beyond the stands of tall trees that now looked more like the bars of a prison. He could not see a way out of the forest. A wind had sprung up that had covered his ski tracks under drifting snow and prompted the temperature to plummet.

With no clear direction back, he thought of following deeper reindeer tracks towards his ski slope and home, but none could be found. Deciding to follow the white reindeer in the hope that it might lead him to somewhere safe, he became more distressed when the reindeer was nowhere to be seen. Standing completely still in a clearing in the forest, Olaf came to the realisation that he was hopelessly lost. This, his greatest fear, was awakened to tower over him. He felt a sickening dread in the pit of his stomach, all the more crushing for it being the price of mindless curiosity.

Olaf managed to bury his impulse to panic, but it was a shallow grave he dug. Along with the many frantic thoughts vying in his head, he noticed something out of the corner of his eye. Turning and glancing quickly here and there, he at first saw nothing – then, a movement among the trees in front of him and another to the side. It now seemed there was movement everywhere.

Panic resurrected as a large, grey wolf emerged from the forest directly in front of him. Another appeared, then another and another until he found himself at the centre of a circle of silent predators. Forgetting his fear of being lost, he was now terrified. Guessing the big grey wolf baring its teeth was the leader, he struggled to put out of his mind the image of being the lone prey of a pack of ravenous wolves. He had never felt so alone.

Striving to gather the need to be both calm and ready to fight, he inhaled a long, slow breath. He closed his eyes. His mind raced. His head was spinning as he was unexpectedly captured by the feeling that he had left his frame on the snow to hover high above the circle of silent killers. Surveying the scene below, he became calm, detached, rational. There was no tree near enough to climb, no weapon to clutch, no passing hunter to save him, no obvious plan of escape. Thoughts that had never occupied his young mind took hold. Shrouded memories swirled in his head. Memories from before he could remember, memories from before he was born.

A jumble of faces and events that were unknown yet somehow familiar flickered before his eyes. A dragon guarding a hoard of gold, repetitive chants yodelling from within a tent, the wreck of an ancient ship stuck fast in the ice, carnage strewn on the snow from attacks on fleeing villagers, a gold ring dancing across a drum. Something deep inside him was changing as a moment of weightlessness signalled that he was falling back to occupy his body.

A surge of green glinted in his eyes as they opened to look again at the alpha wolf. To Olaf, it now appeared as a beautifully terrifying creature. Olaf's face displayed a newfound composure as he stared defiantly. As his eyes met the stare from the predator's unblinking amber eyes, the wolf abruptly flinched before it cowered into whimpering submission. Looking around, Olaf could see the whole pack melting away with the same stealth it had appeared.

Flummoxed and overwhelmed, he wasted no time wondering what had just taken place. His calm determination deserted him as quickly as it had appeared. Putting as much distance as he could between himself and that clearing was his only thought. He fled through the forest, not with the rhythmic grace of a skilful skier but with the adrenaline-fuelled scamper of a deranged novice, until, exhausted, he fell onto the snow gasping as the dry, frozen air ravaged his lungs.

There was no time to recover. A feeling that the ordeal was not yet over took hold of him. Looking up, he found the same white reindeer standing directly over him, a large beast with sharp, menacing antlers. Again, Olaf was in disarray. His mind raced and lurched.

It is a wild reindeer, he thought. *Why is it stalking me? Will it attack? Can my exhausted body ski fast enough to escape?* He slowly stood and looked directly at the beast. Their eyes met. Holding its ground, this beast did not cringe into submission but stared back defiantly.

"Well, that didn't work."

Both boy and beast were locked in a dual piercing stare. Olaf stood perfectly still, believing the slightest of movements might disrupt their fragile truce and invite a deadly onslaught. He remained motionless until he was wrestled from his trance by Bodin and the reindeer herders who chanced upon him.

FOUR

THE DRUM

Áki sat in the tent with his son, Sten, and two other herders, Bodin and Bani, warming his hands. Without moving his eyes from the mesmerising flicker of flames, he spoke.

"Bodin, we have come far and the days are short. Tomorrow, should we again search for our straying reindeer, or abandon them and return to our families?"

Áki was taller than the other herders and a skilful, proud hunter who was accepted as the leader of the group. Despite his experience, however, he respected the Seer's powers and always asked for his guidance in making important decisions. Bodin again picked up his drum. Olaf glanced around the tent at the faces of the herders barely visible in the dying firelight. A look of awe had crept across their faces.

Olaf was again drawn to the Seer's drum. Its tightly stretched skin was made of reindeer hide and decorated with runic symbols borrowed from ancient seafarers, symbols that only Bodin could fully interpret. The wooden sides of the drum were covered with strange patterns from which the teeth of wolves hung. Bodin removed the gold ring from his finger. Andvaranaut, the ring of ancient Norse gold with its growling wolf motif, had been handed down to the Seers of each generation for a millennium. He placed the ring at the very centre of the drum, then picked up his hammer, which was fashioned from an antler.

The Seer hit the drum again and again, making the ring jump from one symbol to another until it remained on one runic symbol only and would not move. He then stared trance-like at the symbol encircled by the gold ring for several minutes before speaking.

"We must set out to look for the stray reindeer before the sun shows itself tomorrow," Bodin then said.

"Tomorrow? But what about the boy?" Áki queried. "What will we do with the boy?"

Olaf looked at them both in turn and thought, *yes, what will you do with me?*

"He can come with us," Bodin replied. "After all, you have brought Sten along and he is younger than this South boy."

"That's different, Bodin. Sten is one of us and has been trained in how to …"

A quiet voice interrupted. "You will find your missing reindeer in the hills beyond my family's feriehus. You can take me there on your way." It was the first time Olaf had spoken since he had entered the Seer's tent.

"The boy cannot know where the stray reindeer are," Áki objected.

"But the drum took me there. I saw them," explained Olaf.

"Bodin, the boy insults us," protested Áki in a booming voice. "He cannot know our ways. *He* is no Seer! He speaks out of turn.

There was a shocked silence. It was unusual for any of their clan to raise their voice.

All eyes turned to Bodin, who spoke quietly, slowly and deliberately.

"The boy tells the truth. What he has told us is what the drum revealed."

A hushed gasp among the herders was followed by hurried whispers. Then, abrupt silence.

All eyes were now on Olaf as Bodin asked, "How could you know that?"

Olaf felt uncomfortable, embarrassed. "I don't know. I was watching the ring dance on the drum, and when it stopped, I started daydreaming. I couldn't help it. I saw my feriehus, and beyond that, stray reindeer wandering into the hills."

"It would seem the boy has the powers of a Seer," Bodin said. "And at such a young age."

"But he is not one of us," Áki insisted. "He cannot begin to know the ancient ways of a Seer."

"He may be the one we have been waiting for. The one who is sent," Bodin replied.

"But why would *he* be sent. Why do we need this … this *boy*?" growled Áki.

"Áki," said Bodin, but in truth, speaking to the boy's ears. "You well know that I am the last Seer, the last one who has knowledge of that ancient craft, knowledge from a time before the Christians came to kill our Seer ancestors so we would forget. But it is they who have forgotten. The South have no memory of the domain of the forest, the life-force of the forest. They know only the realm of men. This is why they have no respect for us, no respect for where we live and how we live. This is why they look only to themselves and take more than they need, more than the forest can give. This is why our traditions, our way of life, may soon be overwhelmed. And that is why this stranger has been sent to us."

Áki rose to his feet and pointed at Olaf sitting by the flame. "How can he be the sent one, an outsider, a child?"

Bodin pointedly turned to speak directly to Olaf. "Tell me how you came to be lost in the forest."

Olaf explained how he had outgrown his skis and been given a new pair as a Christmas present. He told of how keen he had been to try them out, and, after waiting impatiently for a snowstorm to pass, had skied into the forest where he saw a curious reindeer.

Áki protested, "See Bodin, he lies. There was no reindeer within miles of him. We have been searching for our straying reindeer for days and there was no sign of them near the boy."

"Áki is right," Bodin said. "You talk of a reindeer but there was no sign of one."

Olaf felt confused and friendless, feelings that quickly gave way to irritation that he was not being believed.

"But there *was* a reindeer, and it was still there when you came. You must have seen it!"

Bodin slowly nodded.

"Was there something different about this reindeer?"

"Yes!" Olaf had lost the shyness that usually chaperoned his contact with strangers. "The reindeer was like no other I have seen. It was pure white, and it seemed to be controlling me, drawing me further and further into the forest. When you arrived, it had me in a trance. I could not move!"

Bodin nodded again. "It is as told by the drum of my grandfather, Harkon the Loud. The reindeer, Herinn, an Underworld spirit from our ancient home by the White Sea, was sent here to bring the boy to us. Just as it enticed some of our herd to stray and lure us south to the boy. I now see why the drum refused to reveal the whereabouts of our straying reindeer until now. If we had found our reindeer and returned to our families, we would not have been here to rescue the boy."

"And another strange thing happened," Olaf continued eagerly. "I tried to follow the reindeer's hoofprints but there were none. At first, I thought it was because of the drifting snow, but when I looked at where the reindeer had just been walking, I noticed it was leaving no prints in the snow at all."

"So, it is true," Áki said. "The ancient Stórmenska knew the reindeer spirit Herinn can mystically appear to some and not others, then vanish entirely. And it never leaves hoofprints in the snow."

Áki's blustering had reduced to a mumble. He quickly sat, realising that standing over the boy-Seer showed a lack of respect. The herders studied Olaf as if seeing him for the first time.

Sensing a question was about to burst from Olaf, Bodin gently raised a silencing hand.

"Many winters ago, when I was a boy, my father told me of Harkon the Loud's prophecy. It told of what we must do to keep our Stórmenska spirit safe from the greed of the South. He foretold of the old ways dying if not for a Keeper who will be sent to us. One who is young but wise, cautious but courageous, innocent but knowledgeable. An outsider, but one of us. It is he who will safeguard our ancient spirit, our life-force and hopes for our future."

Bodin paused for a moment to look at Olaf, then continued.

"The Keeper would be one who knows the ways of the South and to secure our future must forsake all contact with us to quietly withdraw to the farthest reaches of the world. The prophecy speaks of more than one hundred years before our guiding spirit can be safely returned to our people and reawakened. If our Stórmenska life-force is lost, our people will forever forget the ways of the forest and be condemned to the ways of men."

"You think I am this Keeper? What am I meant to be keeping?"

Bodin started to speak, paused to pointedly look across to one of the herders, then shrugged his shoulders.

"You'll see." Then, to the herders, "Leave us. The boy has much to learn, and we have only this night."

As the herders left to sleep in their own tent, Bodin turned to Olaf.

"You know some of your ancestors are from the far North, and it is to that part of you I will now speak. Despite what you may have been told, it is not Sámi blood that runs through your veins. Your great-grandmother, Tua, a survivor of the Mann-fell, was of our Stórmenska blood, our Stórmenska spirit. There is much to explain. If you are to better understand our ways, we must not sleep during the long darkness tonight."

"Why must I learn your ways?"

"You'll see," Bodin said quietly, then, nodding his head, repeated, "You'll see."

———— ✖•✖ ————

In the pre-dawn light, the herders woke to the sound of the drum and made their way to Bodin's tent. As they entered, they saw Olaf kneeling on one knee with the drum balanced on the other in the fashion of a Stórmenska Seer. Bodin had fallen asleep. After covering him, Olaf had continued to practice his new craft.

The cold air and spindrift that entered the tent with the herders woke Bodin.

"I feel like I have only slept for a few minutes," he said sluggishly.

"You have, Meister," chuckled Olaf.

"I can no longer claim to be your teacher, Olaf. Your gift as a Seer may be greater than mine, despite your age. But don't get ahead of yourself. You still have much to learn … and much to do."

"My son, Sten, and I will go with the boy-Seer to find his feriehus," volunteered Áki. "And along the way, I will guard him with my life as if he were my own son." Áki welcomed an opportunity to offer his considerable skills to help Olaf, even if it meant exaggerating the dangers of the forest a little.

"That will not be necessary," Bodin replied, throwing off his reindeer-skin blanket and sitting up. "No wolf can harm this young Seer. They have already been introduced to him and know who … and what he is. Besides, I have been planning this day for many years. Young Olaf shall find his own way to his feriehus."

"How?" Olaf asked.

"You'll see."

After eating together, Bodin, Olaf, Áki and his son, Sten, readied themselves to set out for a destination known only to Bodin. Sten would ride with his father on their reindeer-drawn sled and Olaf on Bodin's sled. They left the remaining herdsman, Bani, behind to tend the herd. Bani wished them well in an off-handed, seemingly disinterested, way as he busied himself packing tobacco into his pipe.

"Where are we going?" Áki asked.

"You'll see," answered Bodin. "Herinn had our straying reindeer lure us south for reasons beyond finding the boy."

Several hours passed before they stopped on the far shore of a frozen lake. Bodin retrieved an old, weathered spade wedged between two boulders, and taking turns with Áki, began to dig. First, they dug through snow and moss, then a thick layer of sand put there by Bodin so the ground would not freeze hard in winter. Finally, they dug through dry earth until Áki hit something solid.

"That will be the rocks I put there to discourage anyone from digging further," Bodin said. "We will have to dig them out and keep digging."

In time, only the spade could be seen as it threw up clumps of soil onto a growing dark mound on the snow.

"You took no chances when you hid it," Olaf remarked. "What is it?"

"You'll see," replied Bodin. "But you're right. I took no chances. I even placed an ancient curse on anyone who would try to take the most valued possession we have in our keeping. Or should I say ... that *you* will now have in *your* keeping."

FIVE

THE CURSE

"What ancient curse? If I am to be the Keeper, do I need to know about this curse?"

"Well, there is time enough to tell you, "Bodin said. "Áki doesn't know it, but there is still quite a way to dig. He is younger and stronger than me, so he can dig and I will talk … Ever since we received parting gifts from Harald Fairhair the Viking a millennium ago, his ancient gold ring, Andvaranaut, has instructed every Seer on how to summon the curse. The sagas tell us the curse goes back to antiquity, to Andvari, the dwarf. Andvari possessed a magical ring that helped him find gold. When the ring and his cache of gold were stolen, he put a curse, cast by the ring, on all those who profited from the theft. Fafnir the Greedy put an end to his own father to get his hands on the stolen gold. He then took the shape of a dragon to guard it deep in a cave. Fafnir, like his father, was also slain. The ring's curse had done its work. When Andvari's hoard of gold was recovered, the magic ring, Andvaranaut, was gifted to a shield maiden."

Bodin took a moment to check on Aki's progress digging, then continued.

"My grandfather, Harkon the Loud, was the last Seer to awaken the curse."

"Why is he called Harkon the Loud," Olaf interrupted.

"Olaf, some are by their nature softy spoken; Harkon was not one of them. When he approached, you could always hear him before you could see him. He wasn't given that name. He earnt it."

"Back to the story of the ring and the curse," Bodin said in a tone of contrived annoyance at being interrupted. "When Harkon grew old and the Sunnan had forgotten about his mysterious shapeshifting escape from their jail many years before, he emerged from hiding in the wilderness to sell his reindeer herd. He intended to use the gold coins he got from the sale to build a place to settle. The cabin Harkon planned to build was going to be shared with his long-lost daughter, Tua, and the South man she had married. In the meantime, he decided he would hide his money by burying it."

Bodin sat on the edge of his sled and sighed. The effort of digging, at his age, had made him weary. Young Sten sat next to Bodin and leant against him. He did not know the tale of the curse and was excited to hear it.

"A character known as Vándr the Skulk started shadowing Harkon, hoping to discover where he would hide his gold coins. And Olaf, before your curiosity interrupts me again, he was called Vándr the Skulk for reasons which will become clear. Be patient. Vándr was Stórmenska, but never in his own mind was he really one of us. He was a Vansi. The whole Vansi family, ancestors and descendants alike, all rejected our tradition of compassion and sharing. From ancient times the family belonged to the cult of Fafnir the Dragon. Vándr was in the clutches of the cult, never sharing with others, always dishonest, greedy and destructive. Even with only one good eye, Harkon was very aware of Vándr's constant skulking about by the smell of his pipe tobacco, so he decided to put Andvari's curse on the gold coins. He then placed them in a wooden box that he buried in a deep hole, putting rocks into the hole as I have done here. But Vándr, with the patience of a predator, was skulking and watching still. After waiting some weeks, he returned to steal the box. He knew people would become suspicious if he suddenly became rich, so he hid it and waited."

There was a brief silence.

"Don't stop now. What happened next?" Olaf pressed.

"Vándr was one of those herders who took his reindeer to an island off the coast for summer grazing. The reindeer's buoyant hollow fur and wide paddling hooves meant they could swim the considerable distance to a secluded island where there were few, if any prying eyes to scrutinise the true ownership of the reindeer that made up 'his' herd. He always wanted a better, bigger boat to get to and from the islands. As summer approached, he went to a remote part of the coast and found a man who had just the sort of boat he wanted. Even though the money belonged to a powerful Seer, no spell had overcome him, and he was now far away. He had waited long enough. It was time to start spending the gold coins. Vándr and the boatman agreed on a sale price, but when Vándr opened the box and grabbed some of the gold coins, he fell into a trancelike dizzy stupor. Soon after that, he heard a menacing, low growl and felt hot breath on the back of his neck. Looking behind, he was confronted by a huge drooling wolf. Vándr took off in blind panic, running as fast as he could towards the nearest tree and did not stop until a broken branch delivered him with a thump back to the ground. Picking himself up as he ran in circles around and around the tree, he could see the wolf was still in pursuit. For the boatman and the other fishermen mending their nets nearby, it was a puzzling sight. There was no wolf, just the antics of a stranger yelling about one as he ran in circles. As his frantic running and yelling got more bizarre, the fishermen's early chuckling rose to hearty laughter."

Bodin paused for a moment for Olaf and Sten's giggling to settle before continuing.

"Vándr, ill-tempered at the best of times, was furious with the fishermen, but he had to ignore their laughter as he stood perfectly still exhausted and gasping as the stalking wolf-spirit slowly closed in. Harkon, many miles away, noticed Andvaranaut glow on his finger and realised the curse had been stirred. At the same time, Vándr realised the curse must be on the gold coins, not, as he thought, their hiding place. By now, he was in such dread, he decided he must rid himself of the coins in the hope the wolf would go away. As he made a dash towards the water, he quickly threw the coins back into the wooden box. He then ran to the shore and jumped onto the boat he intended to own and pushed off only to see the wolf leap onto the boat. Scrambling up to the bow of the boat, there was nowhere left for Vándr to go. The wolf slowly approached, growling as it crouched with a clear intent to pounce. Vándr, now hysterical, leapt into the water. But the water was deeper than he thought. He could not swim, and sank, never to be seen again. The boatman, realising the money had a powerful curse on it, hurriedly closed the wooden box with all the coins inside, tied it firmly with rope, and sent it back to the Vansi family with a note explaining what had taken place. Begrudgingly, the family returned the gold coins to my grandfather. They were fearful that if they did not, the curse might be on them."

"Is that the curse you've put on this gold?" Olaf asked.

"That is the curse – but this time the prize is much more valuable than gold."

"What is it?"

"You'll see."

"Bodin!" yelled Áki from the depths of the dig. "I think this is it."

"You are about to find out," beamed Bodin with a smile so broad his eyes all but disappeared. "You are the next Keeper. The drum has revealed what you must do. In turn, what we must do is be patient. We must wait for the day when the old Stórmenska ways will be able to rise above the craving greed of the South people."

The hole looked like a deep, newly dug grave. As Olaf, Bodin and Sten peered over its rim, a grubby looking Áki, wet with perspiration, leant on the spade and looked up with feigned annoyance.

"Bodin, however did you dig this?"

"It was a long time ago. Back then I was much younger and stronger. What have you found there?"

"Not sure. It's wrapped in a large cloth."

"An old sail," Bodin said, as he coiled Áki's rope and threw it to him. Within minutes the rope was tied securely to a parcel that was hauled up to rest on the snow. Bodin wasted no time in untying the small ropes that kept the protective cover in place. Olaf and Sten leant forward, eager to see what was inside.

"It's for you," Bodin said, putting his hands on Olaf's shoulders with a sense of occasion and pride. At their feet was a sled. Shorter and sturdier than those used by the herders, it was made from hefty pieces of timber, richly carved with geometric and interlaced patterns from an ancient Viking culture and a carved growling wolf's head, the only remnant of the Langskip to survive, surrounded by symbols similar to those on Bodin's drum.

Symbols Olaf now understood.

Olaf ran his fingers over the symbols and motifs and rubbed his hand along the ancient, polished runners.

"Himinnsled. Is this Himinnsled?" Áki asked, as he emerged from the dig. "We were told it was lost at the Mann-fell."

"It was," Bodin agreed. "I have been the Sled-Keeper for many years and have told no one. The time has come, now that I know I am not much longer for this world, for the sled to go with the boy to a new place of hiding, a place that is to be revealed by the drum. I have been so weighed down by the burden of the sled's unknown future that I had all but given up on the boy coming to us."

Áki sat on his sled and put his head in his hands. He slowly shook his head. Sten looked on with concern. He had never seen his father like this.

"What's wrong?"

"Nothing is wrong, son. Look at it. Look at the ancient sled of the sagas. Today we have been given a gift. Not the sled. It seems it must leave us for now. The gift we have is hope. From today, we can hope there is a future for us. Hope for the survival of our language, our culture. Hope for our way of life and a future for the forests we inhabit."

Áki took his head out of his hands and looked to Bodin. "You never told any of us that you were the Sled-Keeper?"

"No one could know. There are always some among us who are not trustworthy."

"Do you not trust us?"

"I trust you will never speak of this day again, above all with our missing friend. I left him behind to tend the herd for a reason."

Bodin turned to Olaf. "As the most sacred gift given to the ancient Stórmenska, it is this that needs to be hidden far away from the South people. They have stolen it once. They will be back, and given the slightest opportunity, they will do it again."

On top of the sled were reindeer skins used to warm those riding it, and a large bag made of the same old sail-cloth that was used to protect the buried sled. Olaf looked curiously at the bag.

Bodin, observing him, said, "That is yours. Look inside."

Olaf reached into the bag and pulled out a Seer's drum complete with wolves' teeth, along with a hammer fashioned from an antler.

"Your years have not yet given you the wisdom you will need. You must never use the drum in anger or greed, or any other way that will offend the spirit of the sled. It is my grandfather's, Harkon the Loud's drum. It will be your guide."

"I understand," Olaf said, although not fully grasping the responsibility being handed to him.

"And you will need this."

Bodin removed the gold ring from his finger and placed it in Olaf's hand. Olaf could see that along with an ornate wolf head motif it was etched with runic symbols understood by ancient Norsemen.

"Is it the lost ring of Andvari, the one you said was a gift from Fairhair the Viking a thousand years ago?"

"It is. It may summon the curse as it did with Vándr Vansi, but for we Stórmenska, as a completed circle of ancient gold, it is a symbol of the rewards that are returned from giving. I have seen in the drum that gold lies in your destiny, Olaf. Perhaps the age-old power of the ring to find gold will awaken for you."

"I can't take the ring. It's not meant for me. It belongs to the next Stórmenska Seer."

"Olaf, I am the last Seer, and you are now the Keeper. It belongs to you."

Olaf placed the ring loosely on his finger. "It does not fit."

"It will. You'll see."

"I don't understand why you chose me to be the Keeper of the sled, the wearer of your ancient ring?"

Bodin again placed his hands on Olaf's shoulders. "*I* did not choose you. Remember my grandfather who sold his herd to build a house?"

"The one who put a curse on his gold?"

"Yes, Harkon the Loud, a Sled-Keeper until the sled was stolen at the Mann-fell. His daughter, Tua, who married a South man, is your great-grandmother. Your feriehus was once Harkon's home. He knew that if the sled was ever recovered, it must be well hidden by a Keeper who knows the ways of the South, so it can be taken far away to safety. You were not chosen by me. You were always the chosen one."

"Where should I take the sled?"

"It must be far away from here, to a place I couldn't go. Unlike me, you know the ways of the South. As soon as you are old enough, you must journey to the very ends of the earth to find a place where it can be hidden for all of one hundred years."

"But where?"

"Look to Harkon's drum. There you will see."

Olaf was lost in thought and, for a while, lost for words.

"I don't understand," he said finally. "Why does the survival of the Stórmenska depend on the sled?"

"That story will be revealed to you by the drum in time. You'll see. For now, it is enough to know that the sled defines us. It's our icon of generosity, the very core of our beliefs, our shield against the grim desolation that comes from greed."

Bodin looked to the late afternoon sun, realising their time together was at an end.

"Your parents will be upset and searching for you. It is time for you to return," he said. "Olaf, always trust in your destiny as the sled's Keeper."

"When shall we meet again?"

A cold north wind sprang up, bringing with it a flurry of fine, dry snow that swirled around the two like a cloud.

"We will not meet again. I am old and have now completed the task handed down to me by my father, and his father before that. Soon I will be making my journey to the Underworld."

Olaf wrapped his arms around Bodin. He had known the old man for barely a day but had become very fond of him. Perhaps because there was a powerful bond, the rare and vanishing knowledge and comradeship of Stórmenska Seers. A bond that also deeply affected Bodin.

"You no longer need us to return to your feriehus," Bodin said softly. "Now I must leave you before the cold north wind brings water to my eyes."

Olaf watched as the three moved off on their sleds. Turning his back to the wind he knelt on one knee and placed Andvaranaut in the centre of his new drum. With each beat, the ring danced, but when it would no longer move, he could see what was to be done. Looking up, he confirmed that the drum had summoned the white reindeer spirit, Herinn.

Olaf looked at Herinn quite differently this time. Now, the reindeer spirit was a gentle creature, no longer the frightening beast that had intimidated him the previous day. But as Olaf prepared to attach the sled's wooden shafts, Herinn reared up on hind legs and kicked out his front hooves with deadly force. This was followed by a show of intimidation as Herinn turned his head to the side presenting sharp antlers.

Not knowing the reason for Herinn's agitation, Olaf was about to revert to his fear of the beast when he spotted a man approaching. Olaf wondered why most of the man's face was covered. His vacant and evasive eyes gave the impression of a ploy to mask ill intent.

Confirmation came as he closed in, running full tilt at Olaf. The pipe of tobacco in the man's hand was discarded, to be replaced with a knife. With not a moment to spare, Olaf quickly attached the sled's harness to Herinn. Getting onto the sled and away became Olaf's sole aim. But just as he climbed on, he was promptly barrelled off, ending up slumped on the snow under the weight of his attacker.

Quickly, he pushed the intruder off and struggled to his feet where he stood facing his masked attacker, who was clad in the garb of a Stórmenska herder. Olaf could not take his eyes off the knife in his hand.

Skipping sideways to dodge a lunge of the knife, Olaf watched the man stumble, only to quickly turn back on him – but not quickly enough. The attacker was knocked down and trampled by unseen hooves before he suffered the indignity of a heavy sled bashing its way over him as Olaf and Herinn made their escape.

Undeterred, the intruder picked himself up and chased the sled. Running in pursuit, he grabbed hold of the back of it and began to climb on. What he then witnessed caused him to fall back down onto the snow in disbelief. Olaf and Herinn were away, as the attacker shouted a pledge to pursue Olaf wherever he went.

Bodin, riding on his sled back across the featureless frozen lake, was melancholy. Lost in thought about the boy-Seer, he was slow to hear on the wind a distant sound. Slowing his reindeer to walking pace, Bodin looked behind to see Áki's sled approaching at speed. The proud hunter was wildly yelling and pointing to the sky. Sten was silent, spellbound. Bodin looked up at the sky. Above them, flying as if by itself, was an ancient sled, and riding on it, a boy with eyes wide with excitement.

PART 2

PRESENT

Look deep into nature, and then you will understand everything better.

—Albert Einstein

SIX

THE LOST GOLD MINE

South-eastern Australia, 1999 CE

Edda took just one step and stopped.

Behind her was the glare of the Australian sun, and in front of her, darkness. In the half-light between, she examined the damp earthen walls of an abandoned gold mine and the small rusting railway tracks that ran through mud and puddles into the gloom beyond. The vibrant green ferns that had distracted her at the entrance were now forgotten as she became aware of a strong, dank smell that reminded her of an old, damp house she had once visited. Moving forward hesitantly, trying to walk on the narrow railway tracks to keep her boots dry, Edda was irritated by the tilt of her slipping helmet, which was too large and too heavy for her ten-year-old head. Her grandfather was disappearing into the darkness ahead. Soon, the feeble beam from her torch would be the only thing left to light her way.

Edda and her grandfather had begun walking to the gold mine several hours before. They had driven into the Australian Alps until they reached open country, a place where only low heath and tussocks of snow grass grew on the ancient mountain tops. Before starting the walk, as they were adjusting their knapsacks, Edda cast around at the mountains fringing the horizon. She looked through a dull haze for a moment before she could distinguish the misty monolith of Mount Buffalo where she had first learnt to cross-country ski and recognise the nearby ski resort at Mount Hotham. The dramatic slopes that defined the summit of Mount Feathertop in the distance were barely discernible, but once seen, unmistakable. It was a peak she hoped to climb one day when she was a little older.

Edda was rapidly confronted by the realisation that it was not just early morning fog that obscured her view of the surrounding mountains. Her nostrils were assaulted by the smell of smoke that was so invasive she could taste it. In the valleys below, fuel reduction burns were slowly creeping their way through forest litter. A wind had delivered the pungent smoke up through the foothills directly to her location, replacing the usually pristine mountain air with a pervasive pall of smoke. Edda pondered the idea that the day they had planned may not be as she hoped.

"How far to the mine?" Edda asked.

"Not far," her grandfather assured her.

As she started to walk across the broad alpine hilltops, Edda, even at her young age, presented a profile that promised to be tall and athletic. Her brown hair, as always, was pulled back into a ponytail captured by a simple elastic tie. Ever alert to her surroundings, her hazel eyes would impulsively dart to anything she detected of potential interest. Eyes that would surprisingly display a kaleidoscope of underlying flecks of intense green when they were struck by direct sunlight. Edda noticed a ridge falling away where stunted and gnarled snow gums appeared on one side and alpine meadows of snow grass fell steeply away to a creek on the other. She turned to her grandfather.

"Why are there trees growing on one side of the ridge and not the other?"

"I don't know, Edda."

The pair walked on in silence, both mulling over the question. It seemed that mulling and questioning were the natural consequence of Edda's boundless curiosity almost every hour of the day. It was her habit to seize observations such as this and write them down in a small spiral-bound notebook for further contemplation in quieter moments. These *notes to self* were infrequent, reserved for the more baffling of conundrums, those that she dubbed a notebook question, and, because she tended to keep them to herself, her contemplations were often mistaken by her parents as inconsequential daydreaming.

Perhaps it was her curiosity, coupled with a voracious appetite for reading, which gave this ten-year-old a grasp of language that was well beyond her years. When used with precision and impeccable manners, as it almost always was, it sounded to others like needless formality. Despite her unintended eloquence, however, she was often lost in thought and would seldom speak unless there was something to say. This was not intentional snubbing, rather compulsive deliberation sponsored by shyness – although it is also true that there were occasions where she much preferred to bury herself in a book when the alternative was joining in unremarkable babble. Edda's shyness concealed deep contemplation that was influenced by an emerging empathy and an appraisal of authority that is occasionally possessed by young people with her insight. Edda was complex and, every so often, misunderstood.

After a steady climb, Edda and her grandfather approached a smooth flat summit that had a small cliff sitting below it. They rested at the base of the cliff. To Edda, a romantic, the cliff resembled an ancient tower that had crumbled into ruins. Each rock was a similar shape and looked as if it had been specially hewn to build the walls of a keep. She imagined that an enchanted castle had once stood there. As the sun emerged from behind clouds, its light was filtered through the smoky haze to create a strange orange hue that pervaded the dull atmosphere all around them. The effect was to create an other-worldly scene that drove Edda's imagination further into fantasy, where she imagined the seasons had imploded and the orange-coloured air was a foul poisonous fog. Contemplating her enchanted castle, she imagined it could only be the work of its inhabitants; a quarrelling King Oberon and Queen Titania with a host of fairies looking on.

"Basalt," her grandfather said, anticipating Edda's inevitable question about the rocks. It startled her out of a dream-like fantasy of fairies and castles, to snap her back to reality. "The rock is called basalt."

He had learned a lot about rocks since he had become interested in fossicking for gold and would willingly tell anyone all he had learnt – except, of course, the location of his favourite gold-panning spots. It was this interest that had led to their walk across the mountains – to look for an abandoned gold mine they had heard about from an old prospecting friend. This friend's name was Alex Mansfield, but Edda called him Santa because of his smiling round face and white beard. It was Alex who introduced gold prospecting as a hobby to Edda's grandfather. Alex lived in a small old cottage at the base of the mountains, and, although Alex stayed clear of the gold mine as it had been unpredictably exhausted – depleted of any gold – he knew enough about the mine from stories written by his grandfather. Enough to know that the location of the mine should remain a secret.

"It's time to go," Edda's grandfather said.

"How much further, Don?" She always called her grandfather by his first name.

"Not far."

Edda groaned inwardly. She was already becoming tired and disinterested in their outing. Her curiosity was awakened, however, when they started down a long ridge providing her with a view over the Bogong High Plains beyond a steep valley. Leaving the grasslands behind, they entered a low bushy forest where Edda was fascinated by the snow gums that surrounded her. Stunted and bent by extreme weather, the gnarly trees had yielded but not surrendered to their exposed alpine setting. It was here on these slopes that they would look for the mine. They searched for the entrance for over an hour.

"Don, this is it," Edda triumphantly announced. "Look … his name is above the entrance."

Don examined the weathered sign.

"According to Alex, the original owner back last century was a prospector called Lyngsfjord, named after a place he used to visit in Norway."

"So why is the sign Lynchford, not Lyngsfjord?" Edda asked.

"Alex said when he came to Australia he changed his name again."

"Why?"

"Apparently something about not wanting to be found. But thanks to Alex, we have found his gold mine. The lost gold mine of old Olaf Lynchford."

—————— ✦•✦ ——————

The cavorting shadow of her grandfather thrown on the walls of the mine by his prancing torchlight far ahead was all Edda could now see as she stumbled through the tunnel. Still trying to keep her boots dry, she hurried forward, determined to catch up or risk being left alone.

"Are you alright, Edda?"

"Yes, Don." She was surprised to see that he was only a few strides in front of her and not vanishing into the distance after all.

"You're not frightened, are you?"

"No." Edda knew that was not entirely true.

"By the look of the spider webs in here, no one has visited this mine for a very long time," Don said.

"Spider webs?"

Edda had not noticed them. Her grandfather had been brushing them aside as he walked ahead. But looking back into the remnants of sunlight at the entrance, Edda could now see hundreds of broken webs fleetingly catching the light as they netted a gentle breeze. She felt her spine tingle and imagined she could feel spiders crawling up her back and neck into her hair. Moving closer to Don, she stumbled over an old timber support and into a puddle. Water was getting over the top of her boots. Cold and murky, the stagnant water proceeded to ooze and squelch through her socks.

"Are we going much further?" Edda's nonchalant tone failed to convince even herself.

"Not far."

"Good," Edda said under her breath. In the darkness, she was beginning to feel the same foretaste of panic that accompanied her dreaded fear of falling from a height.

They arrived at a junction where the tunnel split into different directions.

"Which way should we go, Edda?"

Fancying she saw a fleeting glimmer of light in a bend in one of the tunnels, she replied, "Let's go that way."

After about fifty metres and as many puddles, they spotted the pale hue of a quartz reef in the torchlight.

"Here it is," Don said. "We will collect some quartz and take it home to crush and look for specks of gold."

"Take the rocks home? We can't walk all the way back carrying heavy rocks."

"A few small samples will do. We will hardly notice the extra weight."

Don crouched next to the vertical seam of whitish rock, took a small pick from his knapsack and began chipping some quartz from the reef.

"Look, Don, a ladder!" Edda said excitedly. "Where does it go?"

Don shone his torch upwards, illuminating a long, very old and not very safe-looking ladder that followed the seam of quartz up a vertical shaft.

"I'll get another sample from up there," Don said. "Don't worry. We all know about your fear of heights. You wait here."

Edda watched Don's muddy boots melt into darkness above her. She turned off her torch to see if any light was coming from the entrance, but there was none, only the faint glow from Don's torch above. Feeling anxious, she closed her eyes, and, in her mind, retraced the way back to the entrance. She thought it was easy, but perhaps not. *What if the ladder breaks and Don can't get back down?* she thought to herself. *What if we passed unnoticed tunnels along the way?*

What if I have to find my way out alone and take a wrong turn? Imagining a labyrinth of tunnels, she arrived at the conclusion that being lost, alone, and underground in the dark might be worse than falling from a height. Edda turned her torch back on. *Best not to think about this anymore. Don will be back in a few minutes.*

⁕

But waiting for Don alone in the meagre light of her torch proved to be an unsatisfactory plan. Wishful thinking was laid bare as anxiety morphed into fear.

"Don!" Edda yelled. "I can't stay here alone. I'm coming up."

"Up the ladder? What about your fear of heights? You'll make yourself ill with worry."

"I can't stay here."

It took eight rungs of the ladder, eight footfalls on creaking, loose timber rungs, for Edda to halt. Looking down, then up, she was struck by grief. Suspended in darkness, blind panic banished reason. Edda froze.

"Are you okay? Are you coming up?"

"I can't move."

"Just one step at a time, you'll be right."

"I can't move."

"Best you go back down and wait."

"Don, I can't move."

"I'll come down."

Edda's fingers were welded to the ladder. Words of encouragement from Don fell on deaf ears. Don climbed down further to where he could wrap an arm around Edda's waist.

"Come on, let's get you down."

"I can't let go, what if I fall?"

"I've got you."

"What if *you* fall?"

Edda released one hand to quickly clutch the next rung. With repeated desperate grabs, she slowly descended in Don's firm but unconvincing hold. When her feet found solid ground, she let out a heavy sigh and the tide of visceral dread ebbed.

"I won't be long. You're safe here."

"What! You're going back up?"

"If you're worried about the dark, keep your torch on."

"What if the batteries run out?"

"We came prepared, remember. We brought spare batteries, and we both have candles and matches in our knapsacks. You'll be okay. It's just for a few minutes."

Edda was alone again and not enjoying herself one bit. *"Whose idea was this, anyway?"* she muttered to herself.

"Watch out!"

"Is that Don? It must be. No one else is here."

"I'm going to break off some quartz and let it drop. Stand away from the ladder."

Edda took two steps back and waited. Small chunks of rock started crashing down the shaft, landing near her feet.

"I won't be long. I'm going to get one last sample."

"Be careful, Don … don't fall," Edda said, too softly for Don to hear.

She sat alone and waited for what felt like an age. She could no longer hear Don, and the light from his torch could no longer be seen as he moved to another tunnel leading from the shaft. Edda decided she could not be too careful and reluctantly turned off her torch to save the batteries. She waved her hands in front of her eyes and saw nothing. She had never before been alone in a strange place surrounded by such complete darkness. She decided it would never happen again.

Was it her imagination in the darkness that crowded around her, or did she again see a momentary glint of light, this time high beyond the point where Don had disappeared? Gripped by her inevitable curiosity, she watched as what had been a glint now became a glow that compressed to a shaft of light as it shot down to the very spot where she was standing before it vanished.

This is no daydream, Edda reasoned as she needlessly pinched herself. *Are we here alone?*

A muffled voice came from above. "Watch out!"

A second measure of quartz rattled down the shaft to crash on the tunnel floor. Just as Edda switched on her torch and stepped forward to look at the rock samples, she heard another sound, growing louder as it plummeted from above. Instinctively, she ducked away into a crouch, making herself as small as possible. A deafening crash exploded next to her. Her torch was knocked out of her hand and smashed to the ground. Darkness swooped.

"What was that?"

Edda was relieved to hear Don's voice. For a horrifying moment, she'd imagined Don had fallen. "I don't know. I can't see anything."

"I'm coming down."

In the light of Don's torch, they could see a wooden chest, almost as long as Edda was tall. It looked old, and slightly worse for wear from its trip down the shaft.

Don was puzzled. "I couldn't have dislodged it when I was dumping the quartz. I heard it coming from above, beyond the reach of the ladder. Let's get it outside into the light and have a proper look at it."

"What about the quartz?" Edda asked.

"Aah, I have not forgotten the quartz," Don said with a knowing smile.

However, he *had* forgotten to bring a bag to carry the chipped samples and had to resort to removing his socks to gather up the pieces of pale rock.

They each grabbed a handle, and, with some effort, carried the chest back through the mine and pushed their way through the ferns at the entrance into squinting sunlight. It took a few moments to become accustomed to the light again, but once their eyes had adjusted, they inspected the wooden box. It was black, painted with ornate leaves and flowers and some writing that neither could understand except for the year – '1869'. Don grasped the edge of the lid to try and open it, but the chest was locked, and the keyhole was missing its key.

"I wonder what's inside," Don said, deliberately teasing Edda's roused curiosity.

"Let's see if we can open the lock."

"I don't think there's gold inside. It wasn't heavy enough for that," Don reasoned.

"If we can open it, we can find out," insisted Edda.

"There might be a few nuggets of gold, I suppose. They wouldn't weigh that much," Don continued.

"Don! Try to open it, *please*."

Affecting a reflective frown, amplified by a pursing of his lips, Don spoke as one who had just been struck by blinding insight.

"So, I think we should try to open it."

Rummaging in his rucksack, he produced his small geologist's pick.

"I'll try to lever it open with this."

But before he could attempt to force it, as if sharing Edda's frustration, the lock made a strange creaking and clunking noise. They watched on in amazement as the chest unlocked itself and slowly yawned open.

SEVEN

THE LETTER

On the walk back to the car, they stopped to rest at the same place, below the fairies' castle.

From their elevated position, they were relieved to see that a strong easterly wind during the day had driven the smoke haze away from the mountains. Both took off their boots and stretched out on the grass using their knapsacks as pillows. Edda watched steam slowly rise from her damp socks as she sipped from her water bottle. Don checked his sockless feet for blisters and declared the boots he had recently bought were 'beaut'.

"Do you think anyone will find the chest?" Edda asked.

"No one has been in that mine for a very long time, and it took us an hour to find the entrance, even with the directions Alex gave me," Don said. "The chest is safe and sound back in the mine, even if it isn't where it was originally stowed. I don't think even *we* could find it again without that map of the mine on the back of Olaf's letter."

"And it was safely hidden there for a long time," added Edda.

"So the letter suggests."

"Don, can I read the letter again?"

"Of course." Don delved in his knapsack for the tin box they had found inside the chest. "Be careful ... the paper is old and brittle, so don't unfold it in the wind."

Edda knelt, and using her knapsack as a shield, gently unfolded the one-page letter. She needed to concentrate to read Olaf's script in faded ink.

"Do you think he perished in a tunnel collapse? He wrote that the map of the mine on the back of the letter was to help searchers find him if there was a cave in."

"I don't know, Edda. He might have started digging another mine and never came back – or he might have gone home to Norway. Who knows?"

"Probably no one," Edda replied pensively. "Alex says he had no family.

"Olaf also wrote here that *'if you found the chest, it is only because the chest has found you.'* What does that mean?"

"I don't know. Maybe that's a question for Alex," Don said.

"Don, how does Alex know so much about Olaf and the mine?"

"Alex's family have lived in the area for generations. Maybe Alex's grandfather knew Olaf when he first came from Norway to look for gold."

"That's it, I'll bet."

"Don't worry, we have lots of time to solve the mystery of Olaf," Don said, putting his boots on.

"Don, what's the date today?"

"It's Friday 28th May 1999," Don replied in an exaggeratedly precise tone, a little puzzled by the question. "And it's four o'clock. Time to go. The sun will be setting in an hour or so."

A brief gasp escaped Edda as she looked again at the date on Olaf's letter.

It had been written exactly one hundred years ago to the day.

The remainder of the walk back to where the car was parked was easy, mainly downhill. As she walked, Edda visualised in her mind all the things they had left behind in the chest.

"Let me see. There were old books, a faded picture of Olaf's mother with what looked like a good luck message written on it, a pen and spare nibs, writing ink in a small, heavy bottle with a rusted screw-top cap, and some old, yellowed sheets of writing paper."

The only things Don and Edda had taken from the chest were a slightly rusted tin money box, which contained the letter with a map of the mine, an old, battered diary folded into an oilskin pouch, and a gold ring with a wolf's head etched on it.

Walking down the long, gentle slope, Edda could again see Mount Buffalo more clearly now, in the distance, a silhouette in the late afternoon light. She counted the different shades of blue in the row upon row of mountains – an immediate deep cobalt graduating to a fragile light blue of a mountain still sitting in the distant remnants of that morning's smoke haze. Just ahead of her was the Mount Hotham ski resort and the Alpine Road cutting through the mountains to the outside world.

"How much further?" Edda asked, glancing sideways at her grandfather.

"Not far," she answered, at the same time as he did. They smiled at each other and walked a little faster. As their destination came into view, the sun was just preparing to set. In the opposite direction, Edda had noticed the large disc of an almost full moon rising just above the horizon and wondered why a full moon always rises at sunset. For once, she decided not to ask her grandfather any of her incessant questions. She could see he was quietly taking in the mountain views and lost in his own thoughts.

It was in that moment that Edda noticed a man standing on the crest of a small knoll in front of her, seemingly in wait. As Edda and Don drew closer, the man turned from admiring the vista of the ski resort below and faced them, allowing Edda to get a clear view of him. In due course, he turned his attention back to the resort, as if satisfied Edda and Don were indeed the ones he had been hoping to see.

Edda studied the man. He was a strange sight. His spindly legs gave the impression of being incapable of supporting his large, bloated head and the swollen stomach that sagged below a sunken ribcage. Thin, pale lips beneath tiny nostrils at the end of a bridgeless, turned-up nose were oddly in keeping with his widely spaced and heavily hooded eyes. The buttoned collar of his shirt had all but disappeared under the bulging folds of his neck. He appeared to Edda like a grotesque oversized lizard.

But it was his hair that most caught her attention. At first glance, it looked as though the clumps of it that stuck obstinately out from his balding head did so randomly. On closer examination, however, it was apparent that this was far from the case. Dyed such a dark crimson as to appear almost black, the fellow's hair had obviously been very carefully dishevelled. Rather than being heedlessly unkempt, it was, unmistakably, a contrivance; a meticulous affectation.

Edda pondered the possibility of there being no real connection between vanity and what might be an inducement for vanity. She knew the idea needed more exploration. At the first opportunity, a question would be entered into her small spiral-bound notebook for future consideration.

Note to self: Is conceit not so much a good opinion of oneself, as it is confidence in others' good opinion of oneself?

Edda's ruminations ended as the stranger once again took his admiring gaze away from the ski resort and slowly turned his head. He looked directly at her with a cold stare. With the opportunity of a closer inspection, Edda could see his ruddy complexion now appeared as violently scarlet in the light of the setting sun. Nicotine-stained fingers clutched a cigarette close to his face as a thin, pointed tongue darted and slithered, seemingly savouring the smoke that issued from both nostrils. Edda saw an ominous smirk crease his face as he watched the two walk below.

After several moments of hesitation to allow curiosity to overcome shyness, Edda turned to look back at him. Her fleeting glance caught a lingering image of stooped shoulders heaving as the stranger quietly wheezed and coughed a mocking laugh. On seeing Edda looking back, his mirthless laugh abruptly halted, replaced by a narrow-eyed sneer that caused his upper lip to curl and quiver in revulsion. The man's hostile snarl was a signal. Edda could not understand why, but for the first time in her young life, she felt she had an enemy. An icy chill penetrated her heart, sending a shiver through her body.

Don, still taking in the view of the mountains, was oblivious, lost in his own thoughts.

Shortly after, Edda reached the refuge of their car, and she again turned to look back. Confusion reigned. The landscape was empty.

"Where has he gone? That man up there, Don. Was someone there? Or was I just daydreaming?"

"I don't know, Edda. I wasn't paying attention. I didn't see anyone."

Taking off her knapsack, Edda was comforted by the thought that weariness from a big day and an overactive imagination were more than likely the explanation.

Taking one last, reassuring look around in the failing light, she heard a currawong's unusually loud call and watched as it swooped low to land on that same knoll. The bird's agitated behaviour prompted a closer look. The suggestion of a curl of smoke near the bird's feet was confirmed by the faint glow of a discarded cigarette.

On the way home, Don agreed – with the needless condition that she must take the responsibility seriously – that Edda could look after Olaf's diary and the gold ring. Arriving at her home, she concealed her newly acquired possessions as she quietly snuck into her bedroom. Edda's bedroom was her sanctuary. A place where she could escape the distractions and demands of family life to find time for reading and quiet reflection. The walls of her bedroom were covered with posters of her favourite movies, with one notable exception. Dominating the wall above her bed was a large, framed print of a Magritte painting; one from his 'Empire of Light' series. As an image that had always been there, looking down on her, it pre-dated any of the posters Edda had put up over the years. The print was left on the wall from a time before she was born and her bedroom served a different purpose. As such, it was one of her earliest and most enduring memories and her favourite amongst the decorations that adorned the walls of her sanctuary.

Edda decided to store Olaf's diary and the gold ring in one of two small drawers that sat below the mirror on an old

Edwardian dressing table that stood opposite her bed. Edda called this drawer her 'secrets' drawer – not that it contained any great secrets. Rather, it housed a collection of seemingly inconsequential nick-nacks and keepsakes that meant something to her. Reminders of a special time or place, or a letter from a friend who had become a kindred spirit. Treasured memories evoked by each scrap of paper, concert ticket, photograph or seashell were of value to her and her alone. Little did she know that when she placed Olaf's wolf head gold ring and diary in her secrets drawer, a sequence of events was about to be unleashed.

━━━━━ ≈·≈ ━━━━━

From time to time, Edda would lose herself gazing into the mirror above the secrets drawer. To the casual observer, it may have looked like self-indulgence. But the object of her trance-like stare was an elemental not literal reflection, an appraisal taking her on a journey. Her image looking back from the mirror bore the countenance of curious soul-searching rather than frivolous admiration, the kind of humility needed for honest reflection, not the vanity that paves a way to hollow self-importance. Sweeping notions, such as what it is to live life as a respectful person or prospective solutions to moral dilemmas, were contemplated on the other side of the mirror. Thoughts that at her age could only have been triggered by her vast appetite for reading.

On this occasion, her reflections in the mirror were obstructed by an overwhelming curiosity. Edda took Olaf's gold ring and diary back out of the secrets drawer and placed them on the dresser, then slowly unfolded the oilskin pouch, examined the tattered black cover of the diary, and carefully opened it.

It was not unusual for Edda to spend hours reading in her bedroom. Her parents were not concerned when she spent much of the next day there, emerging only for a quick lunch. By the time she had finished reading, contemplating and re-reading Olaf's diary, she had made up her mind. The diary must remain a secret between Don and herself.

"When are we going to Don's house?" Edda asked her mother.

"We'll go there one day soon. You'll just have to be patient."

Edda could not be any more patient. There was so much about Olaf's diary she really wanted to tell her grandfather. Other parts of the diary, she decided, must be kept secret from all.

She had an idea. She rang her grandfather. The next day, Thursday, Don rang Edda's mother. He suggested that he drive to their house in Wangaratta the following day and collect Edda for the weekend so they could go gold panning together. Finally, Edda could talk about what she had learnt.

"Skip the first part," Edda suggested as soon as they were at Don's house. "It's just about Olaf when he was a boy in Norway and went skiing in a forest. Turn to where I have put the bookmark, where he writes about leaving Norway for the Australian goldfields. It's where he writes about his big trip last century across the Bogong High Plains in winter."

Don opened the diary at the bookmark and began to read, aloud at first, but as he read, he became intrigued and read faster and more quietly until only a mumble could be heard. Eventually, he was silent as his eyes raced across each line, stopping only to turn the page and extend his arm at full length so he could better focus on the words. Edda's grandmother, Annie, had given up telling Don to wear his reading glasses. He did not like them one bit and preferred, instead, to hold a book at a distance.

Olaf described in his diary the long and sometimes difficult journey he had undertaken across the mountains in the winter of 1897. In the scratchy script of nib and ink, he wrote how he had climbed through trackless bush to a summit on a high mountain above his home in the settlement of Harrietville. He continued for many days, mostly skiing, but sometimes walking in the valleys where the snow had thawed. He described beautiful remote areas with deep valleys, clear fast-running streams and rolling treeless plains of snow and ice. He penned that it was the sort of country that reminded him a little of home.

Noting that he was going where few Europeans had been in winter and with no map available, he declared that he would make his own as he journeyed deep into the mountains. Each night as he lay in his tent, bit-by-bit Olaf added more detail to his map of the high country. He wrote that it was on the third day of his journey that he chanced upon a piece of quartz laden with gold. Describing that spot in detail, Don recognised it as just below where his goldmine now stood.

"I reckon we might be able to work out where he went on his trip across the High Plains," Don said.

"The map he made is folded at the back of the diary," Edda cut in excitedly. "Have a look."

Don gently unfolded the old, hand-crafted map, one of the earliest detailed maps made of the Bogong High Plains.

EIGHT

THE QUEST

Edda had kept her secret.

She had methodically read the first part of Olaf's diary many times, the part she told her grandfather not to bother reading. She told no one about Olaf's ski trip in Norway when he was twelve years old and how he was given a special sled after being lost in the forest. Edda learnt that Olaf had brought the sled to Australia to find a safe hiding place – a plan that took him on his pioneering ski trip into a remote corner of the Bogong High Plains. She had made up her mind. Someday, as soon as she was old enough, she would use Olaf's map and diary to help her follow his journey into the Australian Alps during winter.

Over the years since finding the gold mine, Edda regularly visited Don's house, and from there, they would drive further up the valley to the home of his gold prospecting friend Alex Mansfield. On Edda's first visit there, driving down a narrow country lane, Don pulled over where the lane came to an abrupt end. Edda looked around at the surrounding bush.

"Where's Alex's place?"

"It's a walk from here."

Alex's home was in a small glen that was shielded from nearby roads and lanes by the surrounding hills. Approaching on foot, Edda could not see his modest red cottage until the final bend in the track. For all intents and purposes, it was hidden, unknown to almost all. Aside from his long-standing friendship with Don, Alex opted to have few companions. He was content to be a recluse.

On seeing Alex emerge from the cottage, an excited Edda ran to him. She was on a mission. With Don's help, she had arranged for Alex to give her the more intense training in mountain craft that he had the time and ability to give. Like so many bonds that are formed between master and apprentice, Edda learned as much about life from her mentor as about the skills that were the focus of their arrangement. Beyond learning bush skills and snow-craft, Edda listened carefully to Alex's stories of his life and the importance he placed on respect. His views were not entirely new to her, more an extension of her family's values, but with Alex, she absorbed his words as if they were distilled wisdom of the ages. After all, she was an adolescent, and words from valued others were weightier than familial chatter.

Alex told her that any new acquaintance with a fellow human should begin with respect.

"How do I respect someone I don't really know?" she asked.

"Simple," he responded. "Just as a starting point, always think the best of people. Opening with that sort of generosity works more often than not. You are more likely to get the best of people."

Edda revered Alex's advice, even when she couldn't quite fathom what he was saying.

"Always respect, respect," he said. "It cannot be demanded – just commanded. But it can be learnt, earnt and burnt. It's up to you."

The irony of learning about relationships from a recluse did not escape Edda, who consoled herself with the fact that Alex was someone who valued the quality of friendships rather than the quantity.

After several visits, Edda declared she was ready to test her navigation skills by completing an orienteering course Alex had set up for her in the bush. With a map and compass in hand, Edda had a series of checkpoints to find on a circuit that would take her through kilometres of scrub and eucalypt forest before returning her to her starting point. After being briefed on the course, Edda started out. The excitement of the challenge drove her on at speed. Racing through the bush, jumping logs and low scrub, she occasionally stopped to check her map before sprinting away. Approaching the banks of a creek, she saw there was no junction with another creek, the location of her first checkpoint. She knew the junction must be somewhere nearby. Not knowing whether to go up or down the creek, she hazarded a guess and followed the creek upstream. She was wrong.

Arriving at the first checkpoint a considerable time later, she saw Alex waiting.

"What did I do wrong?"

"You aimed for the checkpoint."

"That was wrong!"

"If you aimed, say, slightly upstream of the checkpoint, you would know to turn downstream at the creek and follow it until you found the junction and the checkpoint marker. The technique is called 'aiming off'. Sometimes in life, tackling things head-on doesn't work so well."

Despite her focus on running as fast as she could, Edda became frustrated to find Alex waiting at every checkpoint.

"You're running with your legs, not your mind," he said.

"What do you mean?" Edda asked, a little confused.

"When you briefly stopped running to check on your position, what did you do?"

"Well, I didn't waste time. Orienteering is meant to be a competition, after all."

Alex nodded patiently. "Yes, that is what you didn't do. What exactly *did* you do?"

"Like you taught me, I checked my position on the map to see if it matched with the real-world surroundings. You know, the hills, ridges, saddles and the like around me to see if they matched up, but I still got bushed. I thought I got the navigation theory right, but it didn't work."

Alex paused to consider Edda's remarks.

"Putting theory into practice can be tricky, but when you do, they keep each other honest. Theory improves your practical application, and practice informs your understanding of theory as it is doing now. When you said you checked your *position on the map* to see if it matched with the *real-world surroundings*, you might have had the two things the wrong way around. Perhaps you should have more carefully analysed your real-life surroundings *first* and only then used that to inform where you were on the map. Maybe you got bushed because you interpreted the features around you to fit where you had already concluded where you were on the map. You moulded and explained reality around you to fit in with what you assumed was right. It is a common mistake that will lead you astray when navigating the wilderness ... and life."

"How do I fix it?"

"Look closely, impartially, at the world around you first. The saddle you glanced at might have just been a dip in a ridge line. The hill, on closer inspection, might not have matched up properly with the contours on the map."

"So, I should not have had an opinion of where I was," Edda concluded.

"You will always be influenced by an opinion of where you think you are. You must do more than pretend you don't have an opinion. In future, to really understand where you are in the world, you should look more closely to find evidence that your opinion is wrong. If you don't, if you persist with a superficial assessment, you will end up making a habit of re-imagining the real world and those you might blame for its problems to suit your comfortable opinion. And it is easy to do better than that, Edda."

With Alex's guidance over many more visits, Edda gradually became more adept at finding attack points, aiming off, following handrails, looking for windows, recognising collecting features, stopping at catching features, and knowing when to use each technique. After many visits, Edda at last felt she had learnt all she needed to learn and was ready to undertake the challenge of following in Olaf's footsteps.

Sensing her brashness, Alex said, "The most important lesson you have yet to learn.

"What's that?" Edda asked.

"Consequences." Alex replied. "Actual consequences, not always immediate but always real."

"What do you mean?" Edda was confused, wondering what this had to do with navigation and bushcraft.

"The wilderness is not a contrivance of we humans," Alex said. "One of the very few things that is not. You should learn to abide by its rules, its natural order of things when traversing the wilderness. If you do not, you will find that nature is not forgiving. It is not like with your family or others, when saying you're sorry for making a mistake is enough to resolve the matter. In the wilderness, sorry does not fix the problem. The consequences remain no matter how sorry you might be."

"How do I learn about nature being uncompromising, about not caring that I regret what I have done?" Edda asked.

"Bitter experience, Edda," Alex replied.

⚬———✦✦———⚬

Edda's mother was worried.

"It's too much for a girl your age. I don't like it. It could be dangerous. What if you are injured?"

"Edda has been preparing for this trip for five years now, ever since our walk to the gold mine," Don reminded his daughter. "We have worked out how Edda can do it in stages and how to get out of the mountains quickly if something goes wrong."

"Alex and you guys have been teaching me about the mountains and ski touring for years now and answered the thousand questions I had about the high country. I'm fifteen. I know I'm ready."

"I don't like it one bit," her mother insisted. "Neither does your father. You are too confident. You don't really understand what you're in for."

Edda had primed herself for what she called 'Olaf's trip' to go ahead that coming winter. Her enthusiasm had overwhelmed any self-doubt. In her mind, there was no going back on her plans. She dismissed her parents' worries as merely what parents do, a part of their job description. If

anything, their concerns made Edda feel even more determined to prove to her parents that she was old enough and
ready enough for the task ahead.

Don intervened, suggesting that he and Edda's parents
could check on her along the way. He also suggested she
should not attempt the ski tour alone.

"If you are injured, there must be at least one other to
raise the alarm."

If not entirely comfortable, Edda's parents were heartened by Don's suggestions and agreed to the proposal with
only one question.

"Who is going with you?"

Seldom in life do people meet who have no shared past, yet
in the very moment of first acquaintance, a connection is
formed that rises above the ordinary cadence of life. A friendship that from the very start can with some certainty be predicted to endure well beyond the circumstances of their first
encounter.

Some years earlier, Edda's parents had arranged with
friends and their son to stay at a remote cabin on the deserted
Ninety-Mile Beach for their summer holiday. During long
beach walks and time spent swimming in the surf, such a
friendship had sprung to life. Edda had met Finn – more
correctly, his name was Fion, but few apart from Edda knew
that. He was about Edda's age. Finn's and Edda's parents,
oblivious to the emergence of soulmates in their midst, were
surprised when the time came to depart. The two young
friends, now a close-knit team, were filled with despair at the
thought of their time together coming to an end.

Their friendship continued to be forged via the neglected craft of prolific letter writing, a pursuit in which they both took great pleasure. Their relationship extended to Finn being invited on many of the ski tours that Edda undertook each winter along with her sister and parents. So, the suggestion by Don and the insistence of her parents that Edda should not go on the trip alone was unnecessary. From the outset, there was no doubt in her mind that Finn would share her adventure.

Edda told Finn about the gold mine, the diary and the map. After informing him that they would be attempting to follow the route Olaf might have taken based on his diary and hand-drawn map, he loved the idea. Edda hinted there was another reason for following Olaf's route across the High Plains. She stopped short of saying what it was, only that it was more than just a ski tour. It would be a quest. She would take him into her confidence only when they were on their way and alone, up in the mountains.

The winter of 2003 was unusual. That winter came after the biggest Alpine bushfires since the 1939 Black Friday fires and burnt through the mountains for sixty days. Despite this, by the end of July, the snow had arrived heavy and deep, falling steadily in big flakes for many days.

It was time to get ready for the trip. Edda decided that Finn would carry the snow tent and Edda the stove and fuel, with the food shared between them. Over the years, Edda had made a list of the things she needed for a ski tour. The list grew quite long, but as she learnt more, she managed to cross off some things that were not essential. Finally, after checking with her parents, she accepted that the list was not going to get any shorter and the packs were not going to get any lighter.

The following week, Edda and Finn were at Don's house overlooking Bright, a town not far from the Bogong High Plains. There was great excitement in Don's downstairs workshop as Edda and Finn sorted the equipment for the big trip. While they organised themselves and packed, Edda's grandmother cooked a fresh batch of special biscuits that would not go stale for many days.

"Now we are ready to go," Edda said, as Annie, escorted by an enticing aroma, entered the room with a full tray of freshly baked biscuits.

That night, excitement postponed any thoughts of sleep. Edda and Finn crept back to Don's workshop where their backpacks and skis were stored. As soon as the door closed behind them, Finn turned on his torch. Edda took out of her pack an old oilskin stitched in the shape of a large wallet. She unfolded it and slid Olaf's diary from one side.

"This is the diary. I'm taking this with us to read each night in our tent." Edda said in a matter-of-fact way. "With his map and his diary, we may be able to follow his trail and discover more about what he was up to out there in the wilderness."

"Read some now?" Finn suggested.

"Shall I read you the part where Olaf writes about a nasty little man?" Edda asked in an exaggerated hushed voice and wide eyes.

Finn mimicked her wide eyes and nodded. Edda flicked to the back of the diary.

"May 19th, 1899," she began. "On my way home from the tavern tonight, I caught sight of Bani Vansi scurrying away from my house like a frightened cockroach. He is up to something."

"May 20th, 1899," Edda continued. "I caught Vansi skulking about my place again today. I do not know how, but he might have found out that I just struck a huge seam of gold in the mine. He couldn't know about the sled. It doesn't really matter if he did. He's not a Finder.

"May 21st, 1899. Vansi broke into my house and ransacked everything. Tomorrow, I leave Harrietville to head back into the mountains. I'll be happy to be far away from this intrusive, bad-tempered man. I'll work the gold mine before the snow comes. Then I depart for another winter traverse to check on things in the High Plains."

"Bani Vansi doesn't sound like a very nice character," Finn said.

"Olaf had more to say about him earlier in the diary," Edda explained. "He was from Norway, and when he first arrived here, he went out of his way to befriend Olaf and helped him work the gold mine, although he didn't seem to like work much. Olaf and he eventually parted ways after Bani was caught stealing gold from the mine. Olaf wrote that Bani Vansi never bothered getting a Miner's Right. Apparently a mine was far too much work. Olaf also wrote that Bani preferred to spend most days just sitting, slyly surveying others as he drew deeply on his smouldering pipe. He didn't even bother prospecting for alluvial gold. Sneaking around other prospectors' camps that were doing well, he would pan for gold in their patch when they were away getting provisions."

"What a charmer," Finn said, shaking his head.

Edda closed the diary.

"Don't stop now, Edda! It's just getting interesting."

"There is no more," Edda said quietly. "That was his last entry in the diary."

Finn's mind was now churning with questions. *What sled? What's a Finder? What was Olaf going to check on when traversing the High Plains that winter? Why did he stop writing in his diary?*

Edda gazed at him, herself lost in thought.

"Come on, Finn," she said finally. "Let's try and get a few hours' sleep. Tomorrow is a big day."

<hr />

"But Edda, it could be anywhere. It's not marked on the map," whispered Finn, as they unloaded their backpacks from her parents' car in a forest clearing just above Harrietville. It was a small car park, at the start of a track that led to the summit of Mount Feathertop.

"Yes, I know, but what's the harm in looking?" Edda whispered back.

"So, this is the secret, the real reason for the trip. To find someone's old sled."

"Shush. We will talk about it more when we are alone."

"But what if that sneaking Bani Vansi character from Olaf's diary follows us?" Finn said with a sly look.

They looked at each other in momentary silence, then laughed.

Don and Alex Mansfield arrived at the start of the track to farewell the two young adventurers and wish them well.

"I hope the weather is good for you. It looks like a good year for snow," Alex said.

"You always seem to know what is happening up in the mountains, Santa."

"Let's hope you're right about that," Alex said pointedly.

Finn and Edda helped each other put their backpacks on and strap each other's skis together. It was an uphill walk for the start of the journey before they would reach the snowline. The backpacks felt heavy, but Don cheerfully assured them that they would get used to them. Edda and Finn looked at each other and shook their heads. That, in their opinion was not going to happen.

Finally, with the ritual of handshakes, hugs and kisses completed, the two were ready to start up the track to Mount Feathertop. "Keep safe," Don said.

"Don't worry, I'll watch out for her."

Edda was a little bemused by Finn's reply, which implied he was taking on the role of protector. She was clearly the more experienced and knowledgeable ski tourer, especially in the backcountry. She found herself smiling good-naturedly without comment at this unsought development in their friendship.

Edda took Olaf's gold ring from her pocket and slipped it on her finger to bring good luck. It was at that moment she noticed a bird circling above making a racket with its loud call. As it landed in a tree, she saw near the bird a lone man, within earshot but half obscured by one of the tall mountain ash trees that surrounded the clearing. He was motionless and appeared to be quietly and intently listening from his covert position. Edda's eye was drawn to his visibly awkward but deeply attentive demeanour – a little like that of a long-forgotten acquaintance unexpectedly appearing at a funeral service.

There was something familiar about him, yet Edda could not place it. As she stared at him, he realised he had been discovered and began to skulk away. His flatfooted and oafish gait would have been amusing if it were not troubling. Edda could now see the man's withered limbs and bulbous stomach. The cigarette smoke pouring from his nostrils dispelled any doubt. Recognising the odd-looking stranger here in a secluded place caused her to shiver in disbelief.

"Who's that over there?" Edda whispered to Alex.

"That looks like Hefna," replied Alex, in anything but a whisper. "I wonder what he is doing out here at this time of day. He's usually never seen about before lunchtime."

"You know him?"

"Not really, Edda, but he is a local. Doesn't mix in my sparse circle of friends though. There was a time when he would come down to the tavern and bother me about the old gold mine you and Don visited a few years ago. I didn't like his manner much and didn't tell him anything. He lives at the ski resort and seems to own most of it. He's got bags of money and has gained a reputation for being greedy and dishonest. His family have lived in this part of the mountains for generations, almost as long as my family. His grandfather knew my grandfather, but I don't think the two got along very well."

Edda, despite realising Finn was starting up the track, hung back to watch the figure, who, after wheezing a smoke-filled cough, threw his cigarette into the forest and waddled away, soon disappearing out of sight.

"Yes," Alex went on. "That's Hefna all right, still smoking like a chimney. There's no mistaking old Hefna Vansi."

As Edda took one last look around to reassure herself that Hefna Vansi was gone, the noisy bird flew over to Alex and perched on his shoulder to seemingly whisper in his ear before turning to look at Edda.

"Edda, meet Jalwahn the currawong. I call him Jalwahn the Loud. He has been a regular around this part of the mountains for many years."

"A currawong. They do look like a raven," Edda said.

"If I were in back in the old country, I might think the same, but Australia is home for this bird, and Jalwahn is a long-established name here. Besides, ravens don't have those yellow eyes." Alex replied.

"What happened to him?" Edda asked.

"You mean the missing eye? He got into a scrap with some nasty types a long time ago. The way he has not taken his remaining eye off you tells me he must like you."

After a hurried, final goodbye, Edda wasted no time in catching up to Finn. She was unusually quiet as she began the long uphill climb along the narrow track. It was not just the exertion of climbing with a backpack and carrying skis that silenced her; more troubling was the thought that someone may be following them. She found herself looking back along the track to check for a glimpse of the newly exposed, present-day Vansi. She saw no one.

NINE

FEATHERTOP

They climbed the winding mountain track at a steady pace. With each dip in the path, small mossy creeks revealed themselves. Wet, rounded river rocks glistened in the few shards of light that penetrated the lofty mountain ash canopy to struggle through the morning mist. Here, the dank forest delivered the heady scent of rich, dark soil, the product of countless generations of decayed tree fern fronds. Lively leeches on wet leaves somersaulted their way towards the two prospective hosts as they passed by.

With each abrupt climb away from the creeks, the purifying scent of eucalyptus met Edda's nostrils as she breathed deeply and deliberately. It was on these steep uphill grinds that she was obliged to lean forward to counter the weight of her pack. A time to remind herself to look up at the surrounding forest rather than yield to the temptation of slogging along mindlessly gazing at her boots. Around them, bellbirds were ringing, and whipbirds were whipping their familiar calls, cutting sharply through the eerie silence of the mist. A kookaburra's laugh echoed from a distant valley. Although she had left her family behind, Edda felt strangely at home. She was in the bush, and her quest had finally begun.

Alex Mansfield had arrived back at Felaheim, his cottage not far from where he had farewelled the two ski tourers. For the first time in many years, he felt uneasy. After wandering restlessly around the cottage, he went into the backyard and followed a path that meandered through a well-tended vegetable garden, a stand of apple trees, past a henhouse and, finally, to a shed, recently repainted just like his cottage, with yet another coat of rich, red stain. Once inside, he took a pair of wooden skis from the wall, removed the block of wood that separated them at the waist, and undid the leather straps that bound them at the tips and heels.

Alex's skis had been gathering dust on that wall for five winters, but he suspected now that they would be needed again. He put one of the skis into a wooden vice and began the task of scraping the sole back to apply a new base of Stockholm tar. Many decades of practice meant he could perform the task without concentrating. This was just as well, because, as he routinely scraped away with a steady rhythm, his thoughts drifted. He was troubled. As he finished his preparations, he was rudely interrupted by Jalwahn the one-eyed currawong noisily tapping his beak on the windowpane directly in front of him.

Alex's only response was, "Yes, yes, I know. Time is upon us."

As Edda and Finn pushed on, they ascended into a thick bank of cloud where the babbling of a nearby creek was muffled to near silence. By noon, with every step they found themselves crunching their way over a thin layer of old snow turned icy from the previous night's frost. They had reached a forest of twisted and gnarled snow gums – trees Edda had admired ever since her first trip into the mountains.

"At last," she said, relieved.

She could see they would soon rise above the cloud that had been following them up the mountain. The meagre warmth from the emerging sun would make the going a little easier, and with the arrival of the snow gums and a promise of sunshine, Edda's concerns were replaced with the excitement she felt at the start of every snow season.

By this time, the two were well into their routine of fifty minutes of climbing followed by ten minutes of resting, but now it was time for a longer lunch break.

"What's the matter, Edda? You haven't said much since we left," Finn remarked as they slung their backpacks onto the snow.

"Just thinking," replied Edda in a listless, disinterested way.

"We will be at our camp soon and be able to use the afternoon to climb to the summit," Finn said, with somewhat confected enthusiasm. Looking for ways to cheer Edda up was becoming a self-imposed responsibility. Lunch, consisting of ham, cheese and salad wedged into freshly baked and still slightly warm bread rolls – a luxury confined only to the first day of a ski tour – concluded with Annie's biscuits, hot chocolate heated on a small mountain stove and Finn's purposeful banter. They had their effect. Edda's spirits lifted, and their conversation grew louder and more animated, until, in time, the sound of young laughter rang through the forest.

Replenished and rested, they were soon on the move again, but now climbing in fresh, almost knee-deep snow where every step was an effort. The track that wound through the trees was too steep and narrow for skis, so they plodded on. Not ten minutes had passed when Edda realised that she had left her water bottle at the place where they'd stopped for lunch. Planting her skis upright in the snow and dropping her backpack, she asked Finn to wait.

As she scampered and slid her way down the track into the rising clouds, she scolded herself for being careless. She knew that every bit of equipment was essential, and looking around after every stop to check that nothing was left behind was something she had learnt years ago. Reaching the spot where they'd had lunch, Edda stopped abruptly. Among the confusion of footprints in the snow where they'd milled about as they were getting ready to set off again were tracks that emerged from the trees onto the path then disappeared back into the forest. Footprints that belonged to neither Edda nor Finn. The name 'Vansi' was now firmly etched in Edda's mind.

Any composure Edda had felt now left her. Quickly, she grabbed her water bottle and made her way back to where Finn was waiting patiently. Despite her unease, she decided not to tell Finn about her discovery, and they set off on their way once more, Edda unusually quiet.

Early in the afternoon they pitched their tent on the snow in a sunny alpine meadow that dropped away steeply at one end to reveal an uninterrupted view of nearby peaks. This view, however, was ignored. Edda and Finn were in awe of the vista in the opposite direction, the soaring summit they were about to climb – soaring, but not in the sense of the newer mountains of the world. This was no Matterhorn or Annapurna. This was Australia, a land of ancient, rounded summits, with this singular mountain rising majestically among its weather-beaten neighbours.

Edda knew better than to climb the peak in bad weather or icy conditions, but today the snow and weather for a summit push were perfect.

"I've always wanted to climb to the summit of Feathertop, but I didn't think it would be in winter," Edda murmured, transfixed on the peak and the route they would follow. "It has to be my favourite mountain in the Australian Alps."

After stowing their packs in the tent, they selected the gear they needed for the summit. The perfect weather was seductive, but Edda insisted on taking basic survival gear. She had learnt that conditions in the mountains, particularly on summits, can change dramatically.

They packed the essentials in their small day packs and started out. Above the tree line, the climb was easier on skis and more cheerful with the unfolding views of the surrounding mountains. On reaching the summit, there was not a breath of wind.

"You could light a candle here," Edda said, as they sat on small insulating mats produced from their day packs. As recent heavy snow and strong winds had fashioned a large, overhanging cornice along the summit ridge, they were careful not to go too close to the edge and become part of a deadly avalanche. The clouds that had followed them for some of the way up the mountain had also covered much of the High Plains that stretched out in front of them, beyond a deep valley. The snow-covered peaks on the plains were visible as an archipelago of shining islands in a sea of cloud. Looking to the far horizon, they were humbled by a feeling of being insignificant specks in a majestic panorama.

———— ✺·✺ ————

Back in the tent, they wrapped their ungloved hands around hot mugs of soup, while just outside, to the sound of a puffing stove, a freeze-dried meal was simmering its way back to life. In the warmth of the tent, they could feel their faces starting to glow.

"It's time to read more of Olaf's diary," Edda said.

As she flicked through the pages of Olaf's battered diary, the folded map jumped onto her lap.

"That's strange," she said. "I've looked at the map dozens of times, so why have I never seen this?"

"What?" Finn moved closer to Edda to get a better look.

"I was sure the back of the map was blank, but it looks like Olaf had written on it."

"What does it say?"

Edda read the handwritten note aloud.

'Destiny not gold lured you to the mine
What you seek is yours to find
The map is not all you will need
A riddle will guide if each day you read
A riddle will guide if each clue you heed.'

"What riddle, what clues?" Finn interrupted.

"Let me finish," Edda said impatiently.

'Onward and upward on the first day
Through fern and forest to where snow lay

Beyond the last tree and up to the peak
To stand on a pinnacle that rises so steep
To stand on a pinnacle where you are meek

Your true quest you've told just one
Neither will return until you've won
Roam a path both high and low
To tall mountains with tales of woe
To tall mountains that reveal a foe.'

They read the riddle several times before speaking.

"It's about today," Edda said. "We started above Harrietville and walked through ferns and forest to the snowline and up to the summit."

"And on the summit looking across an ocean of cloud all the way to the horizon, we felt small, you know, meek," added Finn. "But who is our foe? Do we have an enemy?"

Edda looked blankly at Finn but did not speak. She did not want to reveal all she suspected; not yet.

⸺⸺≒·≒⸺⸺

Next morning, they woke to the sound of wind howling and the tent violently shuddering with every brutal gust. It was one of those mornings where breakfast needed to be eaten before venturing out of the warmth of their sleeping bags. Their boots, neatly lined up and waiting in the tent's vestibule, had frozen; the laces, twisted in odd, gravity-defying forms, had taken on the appearance of fencing wire. Putting those boots on was going to be an effort, and, once on, they would have to move vigorously to avoid their feet from losing all feeling. This was not a huge concern to them. It was the extreme throbbing pain that accompanied the return of feeling to their feet that they were focussed on avoiding. The start to the day was distinctly uninviting.

Still in a haze of half-sleep, Edda's mind returned to the strange rhyme she'd recited in her mind as she'd fallen asleep the previous night. To confirm that it had not all been a dream, she unpacked Olaf's diary, and, once again, the map jumped out. She unfolded it. What she saw made her more confused, not less. What her eyes were telling her was beyond belief and then ... obvious.

"The writing has disappeared. It's been replaced."

"Impossible," Finn said.

"I know everything about the diary, and there is only one map," insisted Edda. "And look at this," she continued, holding out her hand. On the tip of her index finger was wet ink, the same kind that Olaf had used to write in. The two stared at each other, baffled, not uttering a word. The sound of the wind and the flapping tent was all that could be heard. Curiosity overcame their confusion. Finn broke the silence.

"What does it say?"

Edda read from the back of the map.

"South with skis on a ridge long and narrow
A wind will bluster and chill your marrow
Beyond the jagged ridge climb the next peak
Look over the plain beyond the valley deep
Look over the plain that cloaks what you seek."

"Remember what was written yesterday," Edda said, with new-found insight. *"The map that you have is not all you will need. A riddle will guide if each day you read."*

TEN

CLONES

They would learn to trust the cryptic rhymes.

The trip south, with skis, on a ridge long and narrow, lived up to the riddle's description. Blizzard conditions meant the Razorback Ridge made for difficult and exposed skiing where the two would be relentlessly buffeted.

Edda braced herself for the traverse. She did not like the look of the ridge. The wind had swept away the snow to expose icy patches along the steep sides of the arête. The two were well aware that not edging their skis properly as they traversed might result in a fall. They had both fallen many times in the past while skiing and would think nothing of it. Edda chastised herself if she fell backwards when learning to ski. In her mind, it signalled she was not trying hard enough. Falling forward was much more acceptable.

But any thoughts of falling at all were to be avoided out here on the steep, wind-polished ice. With their heavy packs cued to unbalance them, the traverse required every ounce of concentration. Straying even slightly could mean an uncontrolled slide down the sheer side of the ridge – a slide that would end disastrously when their hurtling bodies were shattered on reaching the tree line.

As she skied, Edda found herself looking below to the tree line from the corner of her eye. If falling from a height was her worst fear, this was a nightmare. Their normal rests were cut short as they rapidly got cold, and they decided that rather than unpack the extra layers of clothing needed for a longer stop, they would simply grab a quick drink and a bite to eat then get moving again. In the blustery conditions, it took the best part of the day before they caught sight of the broad shoulder of Mount Hotham slashed by the Alpine Road at the end of the ridge. It was just a glimpse through a bank of silky-smooth cloud racing over their route along the ridgetops that magically formed just below the windward side of the Razorback, only to dissolve the moment it cascaded into the next valley.

Along with the relief of reaching a wider, more skiable section of the ridge, an unfamiliar, barely audible sound was heard competing with a banshee wind wailing from Mount Blowhard. As the strange noise grew louder, Edda looked up at the crest ahead to catch sight of a speeding snowmobile that had taken to the air and was plunging towards her. Finn crouched to brace himself for an anticipated collision, but the snowmobile turned back to disappear as quickly as it had emerged.

While it retreated at speed back towards the nearby Alpine Road, Finn was stricken with horror. Edda was hurtling down a steep icy slope. Her outer shell of waterproof jacket and over-pants made for an almost frictionless skate on the ice. She was terrified. Her slide accelerated unchecked, as if on greased concrete. Her skis were uselessly clattering on the ice around her ankles as she bounced and smacked her way headfirst towards the tree line, desperately trying to free her hand from the ski pole strap that was wedged between her back and the ice.

With not a second to spare, she gave one final, frantic wrench to release her hand, with her mitten still captured by the strap. Abandoning the ski pole, she was now able to grasp the remaining pole just above the basket to hug it between her shoulder and chest. A second attempt at rolling was needed to drag both herself and her hefty backpack over so she could face the ice. With a determined grip, and using all her strength, she now gouged the sharp tip of the ski pole into the racing ice.

Her body pivoted viciously to a feet-first plummet as frozen spray covered her face and frosted over her sunglasses. Blindly ploughing a threadlike furrow in the ice, she continued to fall with the tree line looming. In desperation, she raised herself on her knees to put all her upper body weight on the ski pole tip. It bit harder as her knees took the brunt of the unforgiving ice, now cutting into her ungloved hand. Her descent slowed as the ice, less windswept as the ridge above, gave way more easily under the ski pole and she slowed to a stop just metres from a likely fatal tree. Wiping the blood from her hand and the ice from her face, she looked up to see the profile of Finn against a thin layer of sun-drenched cloud racing just above him. Emerging through the glare, her abandoned ski pole, complete with mitten, skidded into her face.

"Perfect. What else can go wrong?" she muttered.

With her fear of falling teetering on panic, Edda searched out every available drift of snow to sidestep her way back and ever-so-carefully traversed the ice between drifts. She and Finn were reunited not far from the Alpine Road that led to Mount Hotham and its ski resort.

"How much further?" Finn asked, as a way of declaring they did not need any more excitement that day.

"Not far," replied Edda.

With the backcountry behind them, the surreal contrast of crossing a busy road to then ski to Hotham Resort among hundreds of fashionable downhill skiers signalled the end of the day. It was here that they expected to meet Edda's parents and grandfather. It was also here that they were going to decide whether to end the ski tour or continue on and attempt the riddle's more remote route that would take them beyond the deep valley and up to the High Plains. Edda desperately wanted to continue but was worried by the prospect of meeting up with the very real, perhaps very nasty, Hefna Vansi.

----×·×----

"Any dramas on the trip?" Don asked.

"No," replied Edda, as she quietly but firmly stood on Finn's toes to prevent him talking about her near-death experience. "All fairly straightforward, really."

A night in a warm lodge and a favourite home-cooked meal was a welcome break, and a chance for the two to again look at possible routes. To the surprise of both Edda and Finn, there was encouragement from the grown-ups to continue the trip. Food and fuel for their stove were brought up the mountain by Edda's parents to replenish supplies. Next morning, just before first light and while the others were still asleep, Edda and Finn crept to the lodge's kitchen. It was time for the next riddle to surface on the back of Olaf's map. In the light of their head torches, they recited together in whispers:

'With sights set on the plains of snow
Lies a tower of stone you will know
South to a valley calm and sublime
Pause and rest before a big climb
Pause and rest while you have the time.'

"The plains have to be the Bogong High Plains," whispered Finn. "But what is the tower of stone?"

"It's the one I know," Edda said, in an excited and far-too-loud voice.

Finn frowned as he put his index finger to his lips.

"Like the riddle says, it's the tower I know." Edda was whispering but mouthing each word with exaggeration to emphasise the importance of her sudden realisation. "It's the tower of rocks, the fairies' castle that I visited with Don years ago."

Finn searched and found on his ski touring map Mount Loch, the riddle's tower of stone. From there, they were directed to descend into a valley before a big climb to the High Plains. Once on the rolling plains, they would head for Falls Creek ski resort where Edda's parents and Don would meet them in three days' time.

After a second round of family farewells, the two skiers were again on their way. Edda took time out to look across at a knoll where, five years earlier, she'd noticed a currawong next to a faint curl of smoke rising from a discarded cigarette. With Mount Loch in their sights and a good distance covered in a short time, they heard the now-worrying sound of a snowmobile. Not a single snowmobile this time, but a swarm, droning its way towards them in single file. The two continued skiing after a short curiosity stop but stopped again when the noise from the machines grew alarmingly close. The single line of whining machines sped up to surround the two in an incessant noisy circle.

There was no way of breaking out of the ring of speeding machines, no way of moving forward or back. The two were motionless, each wondering what was happening. There was no point in trying to talk over the commotion. Thick, acrid smoke belching into the crisp mountain air forced an attack of coughing on the two, the furthest thing from their expectations of a day in the backcountry. The riders were, to a person, dressed in the same black-and-yellow outfits with the same mirror sunglasses, on faces that bore the same excessive fake suntan. They were clearly an organised group and, unaccountably, out to intimidate them.

As quickly as the frenzied procession of noise and stench had appeared, it was gone, retreating back towards the resort. In the clearing exhaust smoke, Edda could see one remaining snowmobile parked on that same knoll. On it sat a disturbingly over-nourished man with cigarette smoke chugging from his nostrils as if synchronised with the exhaust from his idling machine. Edda knew of only one person who inhabited such a body.

"Who is that?"

Edda's response was resigned, numb.

"Never mind."

They skied on.

At Mount Loch, they rested at the same spot where Edda and her grandfather had rested. This time, Edda's fairies' castle was cloaked in snow.

"Who were they, those snowmobile people?" Finn asked.

"Don't know. I've seen them around the ski resort before, all with the same mirror sunglasses on the same phoney tandoori-tanned faces. They're like a swarm of wasps in those black-and-yellow uniforms. Don reckons they are all clones of each other ..."

Edda paused.

"The gold mine is that way." Edda pointed north with one hand while lifting her water bottle up to her lips with the other. She was keen to change the subject.

"But we must go south to a valley," replied Finn. "That's what the riddle said."

The pair set off. They could ski most of the way down Swindlers Spur to the valley floor, but towards the end the snow was getting a little thin, the terrain a little steep and the track between the trees a little narrow. It was early afternoon when they arrived at an old hut next to the Cobungra River.

Despite the time of day, they decided to set up camp. The riddle had told them to rest there while they had the time, and they agreed the riddles had, so far, been right. With the tent pitched and lunch eaten, they both dozed on an exposed patch of soft snowgrass.

Later that afternoon, Finn decided to explore the area. It was a delightful place with a crystal-clear stream winding its way through a grassy meadow. Crossing the stream carefully on a slippery log, Finn walked up a slope, following a walking track that he detected between patches of old soft snow. After a few minutes, however, he changed his mind.

"You weren't away long," Edda remarked, still lying on the snowgrass.

"Well, I was following a track up a hill but thought better of it."

"Worried about getting lost?"

"No, it's not that. It's just I saw the strangest thing and thought I should get straight back here."

Edda sat up. Finn had her attention.

"Finn, we are in the middle of the mountains ... what strange thing?"

"Above me, at the top of a saddle I was climbing to, I saw them, all of them."

"Who?"

"The clones, Edda. I saw the black-and-yellow clones that surrounded us this morning. They were all standing on top of the hill looking towards our tent, but they moved back over the crest when they realised that they'd been spotted."

Edda was quiet, lost in her own thoughts for some time before she spoke.

"There is a four-wheel drive track just over the saddle you were walking to. It is closed with a locked gate in winter, but they must have broken through and driven in to check on us."

"Check on us! What do you mean?"

Edda spoke in an unusually formal tone.

"Finn, there is something I should tell you. I should have told you earlier, but I didn't believe it at first or at least didn't want to believe it."

Edda now had Finn's attention.

"It seems the clones are here for a reason. They belong to a man called Vansi, a descendant, I'm guessing, of Bani Vansi, the one from Olaf's diary who stalked him last century."

"Why are they here, Edda? I don't get it."

"I don't really get it either," Edda said.

She went on to describe the self-important ogre she'd seen at the end of the walk with Don five years earlier, who'd turned up again at the start of their ski tour. She confessed about the mysterious footprints she'd found when retrieving her water bottle on the climb up Mount Feathertop, and her certainty that Vansi was the one who'd unleashed the pack of clones that menaced them earlier that day. She revealed her suspicion that he was also behind the incident on the Razorback that led to her fall from the ridge.

"You might have been killed," Finn said, with the tone of a concerned parent. "You're right, you should have told me all this a bit earlier."

"I wasn't sure – and as I said, I just didn't want to believe it."

For Edda, the sighting of the clones by Finn in the remote headwaters of the Cobungra River was the final piece of the puzzle. It now confirmed to her that there was a plan to stalk them, although for a purpose she did not quite understand.

"Finn, do you remember the first riddle?

'Roam a path both high and low
To tall mountains with tales of woe
To tall mountains that reveal a foe.'

"We are now among the tall mountains, and I think Olaf's map was warning us that Vansi and his clones are our foe. We may be in greater peril than I could have imagined when I planned this trip."

"So, do we go back to Mount Hotham resort and end the trip?" Finn asked.

"Would you regret it later if we did?"

Finn hesitated briefly.

"Yes, I would. We must finish what we started, the quest to find a sled."

"The sled. Of course, it has to be the sled!" Edda cried. "*That's* what they want. That's why we are being followed. That is what Olaf thought Bani Vansi might be after over a hundred years ago."

"Settle, Edda – it's just an old sled. Why all the fuss?"

"I don't know, but Olaf wrote in his diary that it was special. If it is out there somewhere, we're certainly not letting a Vansi get his hands on it after all this time! So, it's onward with our quest, whatever it may hold."

"Yes, onward to whatever Olaf and his riddles have planned for us," Finn agreed quietly.

He kept silent his concern about what Vansi and the clones might have planned for them. Sure, he now knew they may be their foe, but he couldn't help wondering what would unfold as the riddle's tales of woe.

ELEVEN

LOST

Closing their eyes, they turned their faces away.

Only then did they vigorously shake the wet tent between them to expel as much of the overnight rain as possible before stowing it away in Finn's backpack. The tent was still damp and heavy for the big climb ahead, but Finn shrugged that off. He knew that it was just a part of backcountry skiing. His cheerful nature, buoyed by his increasing fondness for Edda, seemed irrepressible.

> *'Into the clouds to a second tower of stone*
> *That lies in ruins where the wind will moan*
> *Beyond the tower to the edge of the plain*
> *Past the hill of trees with compass in vain*
> *Past the hill of trees where a loss is a gain.'*

After reading the day's riddle, they were not sure of the exact route to follow up to the edge of the plain. Their best guess was to cross directly over the Cobungra River and start an uphill slog along an old worn path. The going was easy as overnight rain had melted the marginal snow around the valley floor. Within half an hour, they were walking through a thick mist, in sloppy, wet snow that was so deep they needed to use their skis to make any headway. The skis stopped them from sinking with every step, but they did not grip very well in the steep slush.

After tiring of side-stepping, Edda unpacked a tube of yellow klister to apply to the base of her skis. The honey-like texture was designed to bond with the wet slop they were climbing. As she started to squeeze the tube, it burst open in her mitten.

"Perfect," she muttered.

Putting her skis back on, Edda paused to marvel at a snow gum in front of her. She considered these trees a special gift conferred by nature, never tiring of the chaotic beauty of their vivid smooth bark, especially after soft rain had caused their collection of hues to glisten and jump. The tree's cream canvas was not painted with a full palette, however. Missing was the expected range of greens and greys. This tree's display was constrained to delicate shades of red, more often seen on younger snow gums. Edda recalled asking Alex if there was any truth in the belief that the redder the snow gums, the better the snow season.

"Sounds like a bit of nonsense to me. Just another mountain myth," had been his reply.

Edda and Finn persisted with their painstaking, side-stepping ascent. With increased altitude, conditions changed. The rain-affected slush transformed to freshly fallen snow. Near the top of their climb, as they again ascended into cloud, they decided it was time to rest and found shelter from the rising wind behind a cluster of tall rocks.

"These rocks look just like the rocks at Mount Loch," Finn remarked as he sat on his pack.

"Yep, they are the same rocks … basalt, the same as my fairy castle," Edda's voice trailed off, then burst out, "Give me the map."

"You've got it."

"No, not Olaf's map, our ski-touring map, in the map case."

After only a glance, Edda announced, "This is it."

"What?"

"This is Basalt Temple. It must be the second tower of stone in this morning's riddle. Listen, can you hear that?"

"What? All I can hear is the wind," Finn said, shrugging his shoulders.

"Exactly! We have *climbed into the clouds to a second tower of stone that lies in ruins where the wind will moan*," recited Edda. "We are on track."

Heartened, they packed away their water and snacks. As Edda stepped into her skis and attached the safety straps, she noticed a large ball of dry snow had attached itself firmly over her mitten-clad hand.

"Look! The fresh dry snow has balled up on the yellow klister that soaked into my mitten," Edda announced.

Finn laughed.

"What is it with this mitten?" Edda said with affected suspicion. "First, it jammed my arm behind me when I was falling on the Razorback and directed the ski pole into my face at the bottom. Then it burst the tube of klister, and now it appears I have a large permanent snowball attached to it."

Finn formed his mitten into a hand puppet that confronted Edda in a squeaky voice. "*You need to stop blaming us for all your mishaps.*"

The moment of folly provided some light relief from the veil of silent unease they shared.

By late afternoon, they had reached the High Plains and the going became much easier. Here they could ski fast in a steady rhythm across the gently undulating snow.

As a bonus, they were now skiing above the clouds under clear blue skies and following a pole line put there generations ago to assist navigation. They had allowed themselves another two days of ski touring before arriving at the Nordic Bowl, a long-time gathering point for cross-country skiers near Falls Creek Resort.

"I've noticed those clouds for a while now," Edda said when they stopped for a drink along the pole line. "We are in for bad weather."

"How do you know?"

"Alex. It was Alex who taught me the different types of clouds and what they mean. He once told me, if you want to know the future, look to the sky. These ones are lenticular clouds. I call them flying saucers. They don't *cause* bad weather – they're just announcing it. They are smooth because it is very windy up there and they form because the temperature is dropping where they are."

"Well, they can all stay up there. We'll be all right down here!"

"No, Finn, it will soon be getting colder down here too, along with the wind and cloud."

"If you know so much about the mountains, why is it even though we are on an open snow plain that hill over there has trees growing all over it?"

Edda looked at her ski-touring map.

"Mount Jim. I guess as the freezing air tumbles down and escapes onto the plains it allows the trees … the trees, of course! The trees!"

"Are you okay, Edda?"

"Look around. Nothing but snow plains, and there it is right in front of us."

"Oh. Yes, the hill of trees," Finn said.

"I don't understand the rest of the riddle though," Edda continued. *"Pass the hill of trees with compass in vain. A loss is a gain.* I just don't get it."

"I don't either, but if the weather is coming in, let's find a spot to make camp and wait for tomorrow's riddle."

"Done."

Next morning, as Edda had predicted, the colder temperature along with the wind and cloud had descended on their lonely camp. Looking at the back of Olaf's map a second and third time did not help; there was no new riddle.

"What's our next step?" Finn asked.

In the absence of a better plan, Edda decided they should continue along the pole line. Once out of their tent, they were surprised to see that visibility was barely a dozen metres. Heavy snow carried by the wind plastered their faces. Their whole world had shrunk to a two-dimensional white pall with no distinction between ground and sky or anything in between. Edda knew that when skiing blind in a white-out the ground beneath their skis could, without warning, become a steep slope or the unstable edge of a high overhanging cornice. Progress would be slow, and navigation had to be exacting. Their first task was to locate the nearby pole line they had left behind the previous afternoon.

As they followed their compasses towards the pole line, they found themselves veering off in different directions, almost losing sight of each other.

"Where are you going, Edda?"

"West, back to the pole line. Where are you going?"

"West, to the pole line."

Comparing their compasses, they were amazed that the two refused to agree. Finn put the compasses together on a rock, then placed them on a second and a third rock. Each time, the compasses pointed in different directions, sometimes agreeing, more often, not.

"These compasses are useless," he said in exasperation. "The rocks here are tricking us."

"I don't think the rocks are out to get us, Finn. They must be magnetic."

The pair were stuck. With non-functioning compasses in a whiteout and no pole line, they were lost for ideas. Sitting on their packs, they ate some of Annie's biscuits and contemplated their next move.

Springing to their feet, they quickly put on their skis and packs, and then, without saying a word to each other, they headed off. In a momentary break in the thick clouds that were scudding across the plains, they had both briefly caught sight of a lone snow pole. After a short search, Finn spotted the pole again, only metres away. Edda hugged it. Looking around, they were dismayed at the all-embracing whiteness that met their eyes. They could not see any other poles at first, but after a while, patience and occasional breaks in the clouds allowed them to slowly move forward one pole at a time.

As the morning progressed, visibility began to improve, and their compasses finally seemed to reach a steady agreement. With each new pole that came into view, their confidence grew and the compasses were put away. The way forward was now clearer. With two, sometimes three, poles visible in a line, they picked up the pace. Their confidence was ill-founded. They had not realised that they were approaching a junction of snow poles, and the three poles that were momentarily visible were actually poles on three different, but converging, pole lines. From their viewpoint, they were in a line, but in fact the two were now skiing quickly on a course that would take them away from their planned route into empty wilderness.

"We have gone way too far. We should have seen a pole by now," Finn said.

It was snowing again, visibility had dropped, and the wind had picked up considerably. Stopping to reassess their position on the map was difficult in the conditions. They quickly got cold while trying to agree on where they thought they were. With the snow poles again veiled, the compasses – although now working – were of limited use. They could not be sure of their current starting point to plan a route. It became clear to them that attempting to back-track along their rapidly disappearing ski tracks was the safest option.

"Listen, can you hear that?" Finn sounded anxious.

"Snowmobiles," replied Edda. "What are they doing way out here?"

As they looked at each other, their faces said it all. Before another word was spoken, a speeding snowmobile appeared out of the cloud in front of them, missing them by inches before disappearing back into cloud. They both recognised the yellow and black uniforms. Instinctively, Edda and Finn bolted into the surrounding cloud, but without a plan, it was in different directions. Edda could hear a swarm of snowmobiles racing around her, but in the deepening whiteout, she could see nothing. Moments later, she could hear nothing. The silence spoke to her. They had gone.

After repeatedly calling out and blindly searching, she came to the ghastly conclusion that Finn was also gone. Edda was alone in a remote whiteout.

───────✳·✳───────

Edda was furious with herself. She knew that she was the one with more experience. She was the one who invited Finn on her adventure, and she was responsible for his safe return home. She realised the folly of relying solely on a pole line, a man-made feature that could be changed or misread. It was the natural features, the hills and valleys, that were enduring navigation clues. She had ignored one of Alex's valuable lessons: *To get to where you need to be, to find your way, paying attention to the natural world is a more reliable guide than anything we humans might contrive.* Now, she was becoming ill with worry about the fate of Finn.

"Consequences," Edda said out loud, thinking again of Alex.

Edda's blinding fury both masked and demonstrated a growing affection for her friend, feelings she was yet to concede. Her anger sprang from recklessly thinking she was somehow above any wild card that man or nature might throw her way. That lesson in humility had come a little late. Vansi and his clones had quickly exploited their luck in stumbling on the two when they were out of the way and disoriented.

"Perhaps my parents were right after all," Edda mumbled to herself.

Note to self: In the wilderness, is pride peril? Humility a haven?

For the first time in the whole journey, Edda felt truly wretched. The whiteout and heavy snowfall had hidden her tracks and enveloped her, taking custody of a usually sunny spirit in exchange for a dark, gloomy mood. In want of a plan, she retreated to the last cryptic clue.

> *'Past the hill of trees with compass in vain*
> *Past the hill of trees where a loss is a gain'*

"Hang on …" she thought to herself. "If Finn is the riddle's loss, what possibly is there to be gained?"

Dumping her pack, she wrenched it open and carelessly threw her gear out over the snow as she wildly rummaged for some chocolate, craving something gratifying in a desperate moment. In an instant, the chocolate was greedily eaten, but her anxiety was still at a peak. Doing something, no matter how useless, was better than doing nothing, she reasoned, as she wearily shoved her gear back into her pack.

Skiing off, she instinctively looked over her shoulder.

"Perfect," she muttered as she realised that she had almost left her water bottle behind for a second time. Packing it away, she noticed a small, dark patch on the ground, almost completely covered by falling snow. To her disgust, Edda realised that she had also almost left behind Olaf's diary. As she picked it up and shook the snow off, the map fell out and swirled around her face in the wind. Grabbing it from the air, Edda looked at it in amazement. There, in front of her eyes, finally, was a new riddle.

> 'You're the key who is free to seek its home
> The home of the sled that cannot be known
> Endure the loss of the friend you had
> You are the Finder now for good and for bad
> You are the Finder now as a lonely nomad.'

Edda realised what she had gained. "No help at all."

With the disappearance of Finn, being alone might well allow her to find the hiding place of the sled that must be kept a secret, but it wouldn't help her current predicament. If anything, she felt even more remorse about the loss of Finn. As she had done on each occasion, Edda read the riddle for a third time so as to commit it to memory, and as she did so, the first line began to fade, quickly followed by the second and third. Desperate to make sure she could memorise it before it completely disappeared, she closed her eyes and hurriedly rehearsed the riddle in her mind. Opening her eyes again, she was confronted by the sight of a new riddle writing itself across a blank page.

> '*At a citadel in ruins the one that is third*
> *You will be guided by a loud mountain bird*
> *Down gentle slopes to traverse a valley broad*
> *Stop and rest when you cross a fleeting ford*
> *Stop and rest where what you seek is stored*
>
> *Where it is hidden no one knows*
> *Deep in the cave that comes and goes*
> *Where I camped on my final night*
> *Find the cave with a chasm so tight*
> *Find the cave and follow the light.*'

The low, thick cloud seemed to be burning off as the day warmed up, and Edda could now see her surroundings for the first time. She was torn. The riddle had revealed she must find the sled alone, but Finn was missing and perhaps in real trouble. The new riddles were still just riddles. The lost pole line and surrounding landscape finally emerging in the misty distance would get her to Falls Creek quickly to raise the alarm. That was now the plan – the only plan.

Edda settled into a controlled, purposeful skiing rhythm that would maximise her speed without making her too exhausted. Without taking a spell or even breaking stride, she skied over the causeway that divided the frozen tarn in

Pretty Valley. After shuffling up a hill, the very first sign of the Falls Creek resort came into view under a clearing sky. It was a downhill ski run near a naturally formed basalt wall. There was no sign of Finn.

"Ruined Castle ski run ... almost there now," puffed Edda aloud as she glanced over to the distant natural rock wall that gave the ski run its name. It was a distinctive landmark she knew from a previous skiing trip with her parents. Increasing her pace, she began to feel stronger knowing that her ordeal may soon be over.

As a thought entered her head, she froze. Her skis skidded to a halt in their tracks.

"Is Ruined Castle the riddle's citadel in ruins, the one that is third?"

It made sense to her that the fairy castle, Mount Loch, was the first citadel in ruins and Basalt Temple was the second. This must be the third. Her thoughts were now a battleground.

"Do I go there or ski to the resort to get help to find Finn?"

She mulled her latest dilemma briefly before deciding to do both – detour past the riddle's ruined citadel on the way to arrange for a search party at Falls Creek.

Standing at the base of Ruined Castle, she looked around for any sign of life. It was deserted. The riddle's loud mountain bird was nowhere to be seen, and with no time to spare, she pointed her skis in the direction of the resort. Finn was again the priority. As she pushed off with both poles, Edda instinctively ducked as a shadow passed over her. A large bird had swooped from behind and was now calling loudly as it circled back towards her.

"Of course," she told herself wearily. "You will be guided by a loud mountain bird. Perfect."

She knew what it meant. It was a time, perhaps the only time, she would have the opportunity to follow the bird and find the sled. Torn between the demands of two errands, Edda did not move.

Circling again, the bird slowly glided to land on a nearby rock where it resumed its loud bird call. Stuck firmly in her dilemma, Edda stared at the bird, and it stared back.

Edda became loosely aware that she was being coaxed into a trance, but she was powerless to extract herself from it. As the two stared at each other, it dawned on Edda that this bird, an old currawong, had been searching for her. For a brief moment, the bird pointedly turned its head. Edda instantly knew who it was. The missing eye left no doubt that this was Alex's friend, Jalwahn the Loud.

A spell was gently binding the two. After what seemed an age, the currawong flew back over her head to land some distance away. Edda had no choice but to forget about Finn for the moment; she was compelled to follow. Jalwahn took flight again. Edda found herself following the bird, on and on.

Time passed swiftly as Edda skied steadily first south then east over rolling ground that took her close to the shore of a lake covered by thin ice in Rocky Valley. Over an hour later, now wearily following Jalwahn still, Edda found a snow bridge that enabled her to cross a flooding river where she was relieved to see that Jalwahn had finally stopped. She was utterly exhausted.

Barely on the far side of the snow bridge, Edda looked back to see it collapse into the racing turbulence of the river. She was cut off. Any thought of retracing her tracks was no longer possible. Edda now took stock of her situation. The realisation that it would soon be dark was followed by an awareness that she had been lured far away from the resort to unfamiliar surroundings. Her energy had been sapped, and Finn, wherever he was, had their snow tent in his pack.

Too spent to go on or even care anymore, Edda allowed her feelings to take over. She sank to her knees, limp with despair, tears welling in her eyes. Without a tent, and exposed to the rapidly falling temperature, her chances of surviving the night were not good.

"Why did I follow you? You stupid, stupid bird. I could be at the resort right now and Finn might have been found. Where on earth are you, Finn? You always make me laugh. How I need you right now."

As if resenting being insulted, Jalwahn landed on Edda's back. She reacted by wildly swinging her arms to rid herself of the pest.

"Go away! I'm not following you anymore!" Edda shouted in angry frustration. Repeated echoes of her outrage 'I'm not following you anymore', bounced around the valley, reinforcing her resolve. As the bird flew off towards the west, however, her anger quickly dissolved into curiosity. Jalwahn had landed in the shadow of a cornice at what looked like a large keyhole shaped burrow dug deep into the snow. She thought back to Olaf's cryptic clue. *'You're the key who is free to seek its home; the home of the sled that cannot be known.'*

Edda stared, wondering if the keyhole-shaped burrow was beckoning her, the key. If it was the entrance to a snow cave, was it *'the cave that comes and goes?'*

TWELVE

THE SNOW CAVE

On approach to the keyhole shaped burrow, Edda was relieved to see that she was right. It was without doubt a snow cave.

Although it was much closer than it looked from the river crossing, the entrance was smaller and the slope leading to the cave was steep, too steep to climb easily on skis. Taking off her safety straps and skis, she took one of her ski poles and began climbing. Once in the shadow of the overhanging cornice, the temperature plunged. She did not need a reminder that it was getting late and the snow cave was her best, perhaps her only, chance of surviving the night. Forcing her worn-out body up the steep climb, she doggedly kicked steps into the firm, late afternoon snow, her mittens becoming snow-encrusted as she propelled herself upright to launch each energy-sapping kick, a routine repeated again and again. With every step she climbed, in her head, she recited, *I must survive this night, I must survive this night.*

Standing on the narrow ledge in front of the entrance, Edda removed her pack in order to crawl inside. The same hesitation that had visited her when she had entered the lost gold mine years before – a dread-filled experience she had resolved would never happen again – now returned. After taking a deep breath, as if the cave was devoid of air, she committed herself to the icy hollow. Crawling inside, she was surprised to find herself in the centre of a small, dome-shaped chamber high enough for her to be able to stand up. There was no sign of Jalwahn.

Next to her was a bench of firm snow – a platform resembling a large, high bed for sleeping on that was formed to be higher hence warmer than the entrance. The only sign that the cave had ever been used was an old wooden-shafted ice-axe half buried on the sleeping bench. As she relaxed into the welcome luxury of shelter, a feeling of devastating exhaustion infiltrated every bone of her body. Edda had to goad herself into admitting it was a sign of getting dangerously cold. The interior of the snow cave was a haven that would not drop below freezing point, even if the temperature outside was in freefall. But before she could rest, she had to first summon every ounce of willpower to battle an overwhelming craving to lie down. As she forced herself to make critical preparations to keep warm during the night, in her head, she repeated, *I must survive this night, I must survive this night.*

After using her pack to block the entrance, she made a small vent in the ceiling of the cave with the basket of her ski pole. Too spent to prepare a hot meal, Edda raided a bag of sweet treats and finished off the last of Annie's biscuits. After laying out an insulating mat and her sleeping bag on the snow bench, she crawled in. Her mind drifted back to the riddle, wondering if she had been led to *the cave that comes and goes.* Drifting towards sleep, she spotted on the head of the abandoned ice-axe next to her an engraving; the initials

'O. L.' The axe could only be Olaf's. The relief that the riddle's cave had been found, however, did not prevent the unknown fate of Finn harassing her exhausted mind, until, as fatigue prevailed, she silently slipped away into a deep sleep, releasing her from her troubles.

⸻ ⧳⧳ ⸻

It was in the hour before the first sign of light that Finn woke to the realisation that he was alone inside a vast, cold shed. Troubled, he crawled out of his sleeping bag and routinely stowed it in his pack. By the light of his head torch, he inspected the cuts and bruises he'd received when a clone had hunted him down, then bound and brutally bundled him onto a snowmobile before retreating at speed. Realising there was no real damage to his body, he was determined to escape.

After a cursory exploration, he realised the shed was a prison. The doors were securely locked. He turned his attention to the huge machine parked next to where he had slept. Climbing into the cabin, he did not recognise any of the levers or buttons on the control panel.

"It might as well be an alien spaceship," he mumbled to himself as he played with the controls. Flicking switches and pressing buttons in no particular order, he was surprised to see the machine's array of headlights abruptly light up. Surprise turned to panic when the touch of the next button brought the mechanical monster to life with a deafening roar.

Someone has got to hear that, he reasoned. *But will it be a friend or foe?*

Not waiting to find out, he jumped down to throw his pack and skis on board. Climbing back into the cabin, he frantically started pushing more buttons and pulling levers as he heard loud, angry voices outside. Two clones were busy arguing over who last had the keys to the shed.

Finn froze as he waited for the doors of the shed to open.

———◆◆◆———

A few kilometres away in the pre-dawn loom, Alex Mansfield examined the condition of the snow before waxing the base of his skis. A little stunned by the development of Falls Creek Resort since his last visit, he made his way out to the solitude of the High Plains.

Settling into the timeless skiing sequence of kick-and-glide, he was reminded of a much earlier time when few visited this place in winter. Perhaps his memory of deserted plains was prompted by the time of day. The resort was still sound asleep. Reaching a high point on the far side of Rocky Valley, Alex smiled with approval. This was like the wilderness of his youth. Around him, there was no movement on the landscape, only snow gums bobbing under the weight of crusted snow and the steady rhythm of a lone currawong in flight.

———◆◆◆———

Cocooned in the warmth of her sleeping bag, Edda did not stir during the night, but just before dawn, in the dream-like half-sleep that preceded waking, she felt a harsh jolt beneath her. She felt perfectly awake in the time it took to inhale a gasp. The floor of the snow cave was collapsing. As she sat up and began to struggle out of her sleeping bag, she saw that a crack below the bench was fast becoming a chasm. She hurriedly laced up her boots and grabbed her day pack. As a deep, yawning void appeared at her feet, her first instinct was to jump to the far side to get to the cave's entrance and away – only to stop and stand stock still, frozen by confusion and her all too familiar fear of heights. Edda was incapable of jumping over the void to get to the entrance.

Sliding towards the collapsing verge, she resorted to clawing and grasping at the snow in sheer panic. Her hands were creating a furrow as the snow beneath them gave way and her lifeline – her daypack of essential gear –slipped over the edge to seemingly float into darkness. Fear of falling had her in its grip. She looked sideways to the ice-axe close by.

Is it close enough? she thought frantically.

With nothing to lose, a desperate lunge had the axe in her hand. The price was that she had slipped closer to the edge of the abyss, her legs uselessly dangling in space. Digging the axe deeper into the snow was futile; the snow was too soft to hold it. Looking between her feet, the chasm seemed unending. Despite her efforts, she realised her worst fear was about to become reality. *She was going to fall.*

But the expected invasion of frenzied terror, assaulting her body, stripping away her sanity, did not materialise. Instead, in the fleeting moments between realising she was going to fall and plummeting, time stood still to allow a blinding insight.

Note to self: Is paralysing fear of what might happen putting more at risk than what will happen?

'Why has it taken so long to realise this?' was the next thought that flashed through her mind.

She realised debilitating anxiety of what she imagined may lie ahead would no longer be a part of her. It was not a determination to be fearless; she knew that would be dangerous to herself and others. Edda's blinding insight came from somewhere deep inside her, somewhere quite unexplained, unveiling the merit of trading gloomy omens with a composed assessment, releasing the courage to act. In that moment, Edda found comfort in knowing all that could be done had been done, and she was able to calmly appraise the immediate future.

It was her last thought before weightlessness was followed by a brutal thud. Finding herself jammed inside a deep crevasse, she attempted to wriggle free, only to drop deeper into the void and land on an icy ledge.

———————✳✦✳———————

Alex watched as the currawong glided to land on his shoulder. He was very relieved to see Jalwahn the Loud again. Alex's family had formed a special bond with these birds that extended back to the days of his grandfather, and over many years, Jalwahn had been a visitor to his small red cottage in the valley. Now, Jalwahn was there to lead Alex on a journey across the rolling plains; a mission that they had both anticipated for some years had begun.

Their eagerness, however, was tempered by the knowledge that danger may be lying in wait. To keep up with the flight of the currawong, Alex stepped up the tempo of his stride. There was some distance to cover to their expected destination on the High Plains, and there was no time to spare.

———————✳✦✳———————

Finn had almost exhausted every possibility to make sense of the controls when a slither of light signalled the shed doors were opening. The two clone guards had managed to unlock them. In a fluster, Finn leant on the control panel. The huge snow-grooming machine lurched forward, and the clones, who had been listening outside, dived in opposite directions as the massive doors of the shed exploded open. The snow groomer burst into the early morning light and thundered away at speed with Finn at the controls, but by no means in control.

Within seconds, both boy and machine were careering down an icy road and out of sight. He had partially tamed the mechanical beast but was still having to use all his wits to keep it from veering off the side of the mountain road. After ten minutes of tense, white-knuckle driving, Finn could see below him the lake in Rocky Valley. It was time to get rid of the snow groomer, head out over the dam wall on skis and leave the resort and the clones behind.

It seemed to him a good plan, but thinking about it proved to be a distraction. The snow groomer had strayed entirely too close to the edge of the road, and Finn, sensing disaster, grabbed his pack and skis and leapt out. As he tumbled to a stop, he watched the machine plunge down a steep slope. He breathed a sigh of relief as he realised that, despite the mayhem, his plan had worked – that is, until he skied across the top of the dam wall on the far side of Rocky Valley. It was there that he became aware of the distant sound of snowmobiles.

Crouching behind a drift created by a stand of snow gums, Finn watched and waited. A column of snowmobiles slowly made its way across the dam wall and continued along the ski trail that took them within metres of where he was hiding. They seemed to be in no hurry. Finn wished they were when he saw the whole column stop opposite the snow drift that concealed him. He could almost reach out and touch their hefty, ungainly leader and had to stifle the need to cough when a cloud of cigarette smoke drifted over him.

Risking a glimpse, Finn noticed the faces of the group were shrouded by helmets, but he could not mistake their identical outfits. They were the clones. Without warning, a heavy piece of ice rime coating the branch of a snow gum above him detached itself in the warmth of the morning sun, slinging the now-unburdened branch skywards like a catapult. All eyes turned to the stand of trees in front of the drift. There was silence. The clones were as motionless as shop-window mannequins as they blankly stared at the tree. Their leader slowly walked to the edge of the track and listened. Looking up at the limb still swaying and shedding the last of the ice rime, he waited. When all was still, he proceeded to sniff the air with the twitching nose of a hunting predator.

Finn made himself as small as he could behind the mound of snow, not allowing himself to react to the remaining clumps of ice falling on him and not daring to create a tell-tale fog by breathing into the cold air.

After scanning his eyes over the surrounding snow drifts, the clone leader let out a low, distrustful growl and moved back to his pack. Just as Finn felt he could no longer hold his breath, the leader started his machine, threw his cigarette into the trees and shouted, "Come on, time to find the girl!"

As the column of exhaust smoke and noise slowly departed, Finn let out a sigh of relief. He was safe. But he knew what the clones were up to and decided he must shadow them, at a distance.

THIRTEEN

FOLLOW THE LIGHT

Edda found herself balanced precariously on a narrow ice ledge in the crevasse.

Looking up, she could see no escape from the sheer walls of ice. Looking down, she saw that the narrow ledge sloped gently down to the edge of an abyss. The blue-green crevasse became gloomier as it got deeper until it took on the darkness of a tomb. She may have survived the fall, but she was trapped.

One comfort was the sight of her daypack resting precariously on the ledge. Reaching out ever so slowly to keep her balance, she got hold of the pack and carefully put it on, slotting the ice-axe between the pack and her back. But even these slightest of movements caused her to start slowly sliding towards the brink. The frictionless surface of the ice ledge was irreversibly transporting Edda towards certain doom.

Her profound new insight into fear replaced panic with poise in her mind. There was no spike of adrenaline, no scramble of frantic thoughts, not even an increase in heart-rate. Edda was calmly making an assessment. At the last moment, just as her feet were critically close to the edge of the void, she did the unthinkable and threw herself forward. The crevasse gaped beneath as she planted both hands on the ice wall in front of her. While it stopped her fatal slide, however, she was now almost as much horizontal as vertical, bridging the crevasse with her hands on the wall in front of her and her feet on the lip of the ledge. Avoiding one death trap had created another.

Edda's normal breathing gave way to gasping. She could feel her legs starting to tremble from the strain, and she knew that in a short time this would escalate to spasms, setting off uncontrolled shaking, as all the while the abyss waited patiently to greet her.

There is only one way to go from here, Edda thought. *That crevasse will not have me.*

Repeatedly blowing the air from her lungs like a weight-lifter about to perform, and with an almighty push assisted by a prolonged shout, she managed to propel herself off the wall with both hands to become momentarily upright. A swift but measured skip sideways landed her on a flat, more secure part of the ledge. With heart pounding and lungs pumping, Edda did not move a muscle until both body and mind were calm. Safe, but still a prisoner, she noticed further along the ledge from her a shaft of light was coming from a vertical crack in the ice. The sight prompted Olaf's riddle.

'Find the cave with a chasm so tight
Find the cave and follow the light.'

Summoning the concentration of a novice tightrope walker, she edged her way along the slender ledge towards the light. Squeezing into the cleft, Edda was relieved to find it gradually turned into a broad avenue that steered her into a large ice chamber.

Relax, you can now relax, she told herself.

The going was easy as she walked towards the light along a shallow stream that ran beneath a large tunnel of smooth, clear ice. Her surroundings eerily resembled the tunnels in the lost gold mine. Using rocks in the stream as stepping stones to keep her boots dry, Edda walked on and on, encouraged by the riddle to follow the light.

At a bend in the ice tunnel, Edda stopped. In disbelief that the riddle had misled her, she stared and pondered. The light was coming from a large fracture high above, so high it reminded her of the vaulted ceiling of a large cathedral.

It can't be the end of the road, she thought. After all she had been through, she refused to believe that. Just at that moment, the glow above her changed to a beam of light that shot to the very spot she was standing. *Just like the gold mine.*

A hurried search revealed a vertical reef of quartz jutting from the ice and extending upward from the shallow stream. Above, in what looked like a lofty ice chamber, Edda could make out where the light was glowing brightest.

Was my experience in the gold mine a rehearsal? This must be the way, Edda convinced herself.

Feeling more self-assured than the memory of her attempt to climb the gold mine's insecure ladder, she began to scramble up the column of rock. The going was easy, and Edda was surprised how high above the stream she managed to climb in a short time. Almost at the top, she stopped to inspect the final section that, unlike the rest of the climb, was vertical, and, in places, overhanging. After assessing a possible way up and committing to climb, her confidence was cruelly tested. With each handhold and every foothold, the rock crumbled away beneath her weight and rattled down to splash into the stream far below. The slightest shifting of her stance resulted in the decayed rock coming apart.

Edda froze, a strategy borne of prudence, not panic. Looking above, she saw a solid horizontal shelf. It was enticingly close. Stretching a full arm's length above her head was a risk, but in the absence of any other option, it had to be done. To keep her balance, she inched one hand upward, slowly, warily, mindful that the slightest shift might cause a protruding rock that was her one remaining handhold to give way. At full stretch, she curled her fingers over the lip of the shelf. They searched eagerly, only to be met everywhere by a thick layer of smooth, hard ice. The promise of a secure handhold evaporated as the rock around her continued to crumble.

Moving either up or down was madness on the decayed rock. And staying put in her awkward position would, in a short time, result in the rock giving way as cramping muscles began to tremble and shake. If there was a time for panic, this was it, but with increasing peril, Edda's composure grew. Reassured by the feel of cold steel on the back of her neck, she carefully reached over her shoulder for the ice-axe. She slowly retrieved it, just as her other hand was starting to cramp from the strain of its tenuous grip. Inspecting the teeth on the head of the axe, the teeth that were to be the difference between safety and disaster, she decided to chance a swing of the axe to land it on the icy ledge above. There would be no second chance. She knew a decisive swing was needed, one that would unbalance her.

One determined, teeth-gritting blow and the axe head landed. Her footholds and handhold gave way. She pivoted wildly into empty space. Grabbing the shaft of the axe with both hands and looking down as she was swinging, it seemed curious that the shallow stream was much further below than a moment before. Edda allowed herself the luxury of taking a deep breath, her last for now. Slowly exhaling, she hauled her dangling body up with a vice-like grip on the ice-axe. Her eyes met the axe head. It was more a confrontation than a meeting. The teeth had not bitten. Perched delicately on hard shining ice, they had not so much as scratched the surface. One wrong move and the unbalanced axe would peel off and plummet with her hands still gripping it.

Beyond the head of the axe, at the back of the ledge, Edda spotted solid rock. Uncertain if it was within reach, and with her strength quickly running out, she glared as it enticed another gamble. The decision to take one hand off the axe's shaft was taken after a momentary assessment. Trusting her weight on one handgrip, Edda ever so slowly slid her other hand across the ice towards the hoped-for security of a hand-hold. She greedily wrapped her fingers around it and fol-lowed this with an inelegant scramble. Edda breathed again; she was lying on the ice ledge, exposed but safe.

If this is really the gold mine's icy twin, have I just climbed to the one-time hiding place of the painted chest? Edda pondered.

—————✯✯—————

Tentatively standing, she saw the entrance to an ice cham-ber. From inside the chamber, the glowing light she'd been following, now stronger, audibly pulsed in harmony with Edda's pounding heart. Moving forward, she entered the chamber and there discovered the source of the light – a semi-transparent figure whose eyes flashed brightly as she moved closer.

"Who are you?"

"I am Bodin, the last Seer from the line of Harkon the Loud."

"What are you doing here?"

"I have come to guide the Finder, the one who wears the Seer's ring of gold."

Edda involuntarily placed one hand over the other, hiding Olaf's ring, then had second thoughts.

"This ring? Will you guide me out of here?"

"Yes, that ring. The Seer's ring of the forgotten Stórmenska."

"Who?"

"We are Stórmenska, perhaps forgotten … some would say extinct."

"You can't be extinct and still be here."

Bodin stepped closer. Edda could see more clearly the shimmering form of a small, old man dressed in reindeer hide.

"Are you the Seer Olaf wrote about in his diary?" Edda asked, as a realisation dawned. "The one who rescued him when he was lost in the wilderness?"

"Yes, I am he," replied the old man. "I have come from the Underworld, the land of my ancestor Spirits."

I don't know what you are talking about, thought Edda. One thing and one thing only was occupying her mind.

"Do you know a way out of here?" she asked.

"You are the Finder. I am here to guide you, to prepare you for what is coming."

"What is coming? Is this about the sled?"

"Yes, young Edda. It is all about the sled."

"You think I am this Finder? I'm not the Finder! I was just following clues from an old map in a chest I found and I ..."

"Did you *find* the chest?" Bodin asked.

Edda recalled Olaf's one-hundred-year-old letter from the gold mine with a map of the mine drawn on the back, a letter that concluded with the comment, '*If you have found the chest it is only because the chest has found you.*'

"How? Why me? Why did it find *me*?"

"The sled had to be hidden at the end of the earth for a hundred years. That time has passed. You are a Finder because there is no Seer. I, Bodin, am the last in the ancient line of Seers."

"Is what you say true? Your people are extinct?"

"No, just concealed in a land far from here. To survive, we have been in hiding, but in plain sight. To outsiders, we are extinct. We no longer live as Stórmenska of old, but one day we will return to the White Sea and live as we once did."

"With your sled?"

"With our sled."

"Why has the sled been so far from its home for so long?"

"Things must change if we wish them to remain the same," Bodin replied.

"What does that mean?" Finding her way out of the crevasse was no longer the main thing occupying Edda's curious mind. With no response, her need for answers did not waver.

"Why is the sled so important?"

After a slight hesitation to gather his thoughts, Bodin began to speak while Edda listened, fascinated. He took a considerable time to describe in great detail the antiquity and importance of the sled to Stórmenska culture. When he had finally finished, he went on to talk about his only visit to the distant South.

"As a young man I heard stories about a sled called Vansi's Sled," Bodin said. "I set off on a long journey to search in the South following every lead for what I hoped might be our own lost sled, Himinnsled. After some months, I found it in the far South. It was on displayed in a museum as a curiosity for South people. The display included an explanation that it was a rare and priceless Viking sled inexplicably almost in its original condition, and it was named Vansi's Sled after the Vansi family who had 'found' it and sold it to the museum. I was furious that it was named after the people who stole it from us at the Mann-Fell and was determined to get it back to those it belonged to. That night," he continued, "I broke into the museum and hurried back up north with the sled to hide it in a deep hole next to a lake."

Edda's attention to Bodin's every word was unwavering as he continued.

"We are now few in number, but there is still hope that one day we can again live our life as we should, as our ancestors did," Bodin went on. "One day the sled will summon us back to the White Sea to rebuild the life we once shared with the forest and each other."

"Why don't you take the sled back to its home now?" Edda asked.

"We need to be patient a little longer. We had hoped the sled would be forgotten by those who are devoured by greed and revenge. We hoped that greed could not be so patient as to endure a hundred years of concealment. We had hoped those who would take it from us were no longer a threat."

"People like Bani Vansi." Edda was quick to make the connection from Olaf's diary. It revealed to Bodin Edda's desire to work with him in his mission to safeguard the sled. "What must I do?" Edda asked.

"You have done it. You have found the sled, and now that you understand its real value, you will protect it."

"But I haven't found the sled."

"Haven't you? ... You'll see."

"You said you were going to prepare me for what is coming. I don't know what to do. What am I supposed to do?"

The worry written on Edda's face pressed Bodin to explain.

"In this void, in finding me, you learned that fear of what *might* happen may be putting more at risk than what *will* happen. With that, you have shaken off Edda the fainthearted. Yesterday's Edda has been confined to memories of your childhood. You have defeated your demons. You are ready. You will know what to do."

"How?"

"You'll see."

"But I don't see how."

"Because you are the Finder, you will do whatever you can't not do."

"What does that mean?"

There was no answer. Edda watched in amazement as the figure of Bodin gradually grew fainter and the light that had guided her to the chamber dwindled. As he faded away, Bodin spoke his last words.

"You'll see."

In that moment, a violent shock rocked the ice chamber around her, causing deep cracks to spread across its vaulted ice ceiling. In the invading darkness, Edda had no way of knowing how to get out of the chamber, how to escape through the icy burrows far below. She braced herself for the possibility of another crevasse opening at her feet – or was it to be falling shards of ice before a complete cave-in? Her newfound insight into fear was being tested, and even a composed assessment of her predicament found no immediate answer.

A second, more violent, shock took her breath away.

FOURTEEN

WEALTH AND WORTH

Edda sat bolt upright and desperately looked around. Puzzlement swiftly turned to relief. She realised she was in her sleeping bag in the snow cave. There was no crevasse to be seen, no deep ice vaults – and no Bodin. A long sigh emptied her lungs, fogging the cave. Through the fog, she noticed that her pack was still blocking the cave's entrance. The ice-axe and her small day pack were still sitting next to her on the bench of snow.

"Was I dreaming?" she said to herself. "It was so real. I could *see it*. I watched on as it happened."

Daylight creeping around her pack into the cave signalled the sun had risen. As Edda blinked away the long night and slid off the sleeping bench where she had succumbed to her deep enlightening sleep, she noticed she had disturbed a covering of snow on the bench top to expose a layer of thick ice. Brushing the snow off the bench and peering through the semi-transparent ice, she could barely make out pieces of old carved timber. After several attempts to break through the ice by thumping her fists, she picked up the ice axe, and with a determined blow, shattered the ice.

Curiosity turned to frenzied digging with her bare hands through the snow that lay beneath, as, bit-by-bit, she freed an ancient sled from its frozen vault.

"All night I was unknowingly sleeping on the sled. *Bodin was right.* I had found it."

Edda's thoughts flicked to her dilemma – the sled, her new treasured discovery, and Finn, her lost companion.

"If I am the Finder, why don't I know what to do next?" she pondered out loud.

Pushing her pack out of the cave entrance, she remembered, a little too late, the steep climb to the cave the previous night. Her pack tumbled, lurched and skidded its way down the slope to rest next to her skis. A fascination with the sled swamped all thoughts of Finn, at least for the moment. As she pushed the heavy wooden sled out into the light of day, it began to slip from her grip. Edda impulsively pounced on it, and, to her astonishment, they were both away, sliding and bouncing down the steep slope. For a moment, Edda felt the sled was flying, then a bone jarring thump brought her unmistakably back to earth.

Barrelling into a snow drift, the sled came to an abrupt halt – but Edda did not. Tumbling then sprawling onto the snow, she looked up to meet the reptilian gaze of Hefna Vansi. He stood in silence, staring at her from menacing hooded eyes. Edda had not a moment to collect herself before Vansi spoke in a slow, rasping voice.

"You have what I want, little girl."

"It is not yours to have!" shouted Edda – the new Edda, Edda the Finder, taking herself by surprise with her heated response. She flinched inwardly as Alex's words came back to her. "As a starting point, always think the best of people. Being generous usually works."

Vansi was undeterred by Edda's outburst. "I mean to make it mine."

"Why? What could you possibly want with an old sled?"

"It is owed to me, and if I am to believe the sagas that tell of the sled's promise of prosperity, it may have worth beyond calculation."

"You say its value is beyond calculation … You're right, it is beyond any measure of money." Edda had reverted to her respectful demeanour, veiling the glowing embers of her anger.

Slowly shaking his head, Vansi's face began to crease into a patronising smile, before his countenance abruptly morphed into a display of sheer wide-eyed glee, an expression Edda could not interpret.

Vansi had noticed on her finger the ancient wolf head motif of Andvari the dwarf's ring. In one fell swoop, he was about to possess the sled, depriving the Stórmenska of their icon of generosity, and Andvaranaut, the ring once stolen by his idol, Fafnir the Dragon. Destroying the ring would finally rid the world of Andvari's curse on thieves.

"I could destroy both the sled and the ring. Not a bad day's work," Vansi mumbled to himself, then more loudly, "That gold ring. Where did you get it?"

"It's not mine. I have it for safekeeping."

"I'll have that as well."

"It is not yours to wear."

"Oh no, I won't be doing that. I won't be touching it. Just put it on the sled and walk away. A spell was placed on that ring for the likes of me."

"What do you mean?"

"It's another curse. For generations, my family has had to endure curses. There is no hope for us. No hope except the freedom that money brings, the hope that greed promises. Even my very appearance is a curse."

Edda was surprised by the normally menacing Vansi's sudden outpouring of child-like whinging.

"People, good people, base worth on what we do, not on our appearance. That's just an excuse," Edda said.

Vansi, taking exception to Edda's reply, took a step closer – then a calculated, intimidating second step that placed him standing directly over her with a new expression, one of dogged resolve.

"Greed gives me choices and money gives me power over others." Vansi then continued in the same loud, angry voice, "That is why I have spent my life pursuing money. If you took one moment to be honest with yourself, you would admit that you also want that freedom, that power. You would realise you are begrudgingly envious of me, of what I have. Have you considered that you may be arrogant? Do you believe you have the right to weigh up virtue and judge others? Why don't you just go home and leave this whole business to the grown-ups."

Edda paused to contemplate, to take up the challenge of being honest with herself. To deal with her newest dilemma.

Am I envious of his wealth, his power? Edda quietly pondered. *If I had the sled, maybe I could be wealthy and have a better life. And perhaps I could use some of my wealth for good. That would be a good reason to keep it, and that would mean it isn't all about what I want. After all, I am the Finder. Maybe as the Finder I should be the one to keep the sled. Yes, keep it just for me, that could work!*

Enticing as the prospect of possessing the sled had become, Edda felt an involuntary cringe at the thought of explaining to Alex what she had done. She stopped to take stock. *Am I just as arrogant, just as greedy … but for the sorts of things that I want? In my own way, am I the conceited one here? Note to self: Is arrogance capable of recognising itself?*

Edda was deeply shocked by her private thoughts. She was beginning to understand just how beguiling greed could be. From that moment, she would make a point of being suspicious of what she wanted.

Perplexed, Edda looked beyond her routine existence to her task, as the newly appointed Finder, urgently searching for a plan, or even just her next move. She understood the need to act, but the seeds of self-doubt had been cast. Feeling out of her depth, she looked up at Hefna Vansi. He, in turn, sensing her uncertainty, straightened his back, raised his chin, and, with the self-assurance of a superior being, looked down his nose at her.

Tilting his head to one side, he at first gave the impression of making an assessment of Edda, but with the return of his patronising smile accompanied by a dismissive shake of his head, Edda realised he was making no assessment. In that moment, she saw an entrenched judgment, perhaps cemented to the time when, as a ten-year-old, she'd dared to turn to look back at him on the walk from the gold mine. A judgement not based on who she was, but on *what* she was in his mind. In his own words, *a little girl.*

With this realisation, Edda's mind cleared, and she was able to establish a way forward. Hefna Vansi's greed had been enabled by people, decent people, who found it more comfortable to stand aside when confronted by his blunt and aggressive manner. *Edda was not going to do as he said. She was not about to go home and leave the whole business to the grown-ups.* While she understood that sometimes, with the best of intentions, the grown-ups' judgement could be flawed, she was in no doubt that right now Hefna Vansi's intentions were far from honourable.

"If I gave up, if I did as you said and went home, I would be accepting that yours is the way of the world," Edda said. "Many of us have been timid, allowing self-indulgence to thrive, but that does not make greed right. You are already wealthy. You own most of the lodgings in more than a few ski resorts. Why do you want more? Why the sled?"

"Because in life those who are not greedy are left behind."

"I know that if I devoted my whole life to clutching at every scrap of wealth, it is my life that would be fully spent," Edda retorted. "My life would have little value. Why would I want to be a wealthy person with a bankrupt life? Stubbornly chasing money would *rob* me of my freedom, not give it to me."

"I'll take the risk. It is a dream worth chasing," Vansi replied with a dismissive wave of his hand.

"It is a dream that is lost in the seeking," Edda said.

"Like I said, I'll take the risk. Besides, it is more than just chasing wealth. It is revenge. As the last of the Vansi clan, I want the satisfaction of knowing those doomed wandering Vikings will suffer endlessly for the loss of their precious sled. I want the so-called spirit of the sled lost to the world forever. I will have the sled ... now!"

Edda was incensed at the possibility of losing the sled. She understood its importance and knew what she must do – or as Bodin had said, what she couldn't *not* do. Vansi's ongoing posturing and scornful banter may have been designed to intimidate Edda into conceding defeat, but, instead, it had provided clarity. A clarity that shaped in her mind who she was by realising who she was not, nor could ever be. Uttering strangely familiar words in a slow, strident voice, Edda spoke.

"None shall have the sled. None but those it belongs to."

"Oh, I do believe I *will* have it," replied Vansi in a tone stained with self-importance. "You can't see it can you, little girl? One day you will realise life is a competition and I'm about to win."

"If you truly believe life is as simple as a competition, you have already lost. The sled is not about the value it has to you. It's not about winning. It is stealing the rebirth of an ancient people. Their future, their very reason to hope, may be gone with the loss of the sled."

"Not my problem," muttered Vansi.

The snow that had dusted Edda after skidding off the sled was melting away, leaving wet hair still partly obscuring her face. Vansi caught a glimpse for the first time, of eyes staring from behind dripping strands. He was startled. As Edda's smouldering determination met his gaze, his mouth gaped open. His bewildered bearing revealed the realisation he was dealing with someone quite unexpected. Mistaking Edda's respectful shyness for childlike meekness, he had confused it with weakness, just as his own posturing banter had revealed his confusion between belligerence and strength.

Edda's glowing embers burst into flames. There was no display of anger, no shouting. She spoke in a respectful, measured tone that had the effect of being much more unnerving.

"Have you considered that the sled's promise of prosperity is not about wealth, that the sled as an icon of generosity is not about unstintingly providing riches for you?"

"I don't understand. What else could the sled's promise be about?" Vansi asked with a look of genuine confusion.

"Maybe the people the sled belongs to are prosperous in having the rewards of sharing and mutual generosity. The rewards of a peaceful existence, by having a fulfilled life where they are free from the scourge of greed. Maybe the sled's promise of prosperity has nothing at all to do with what you can measure with money."

"Nothing is beyond measuring with money," spat a rasping reply. "If that's all prosperity means to them, they don't really need the sled. But I still want it. It still has to be worth something."

"You would sell it?" Edda asked incredulously.

"Of course I would sell it! A museum would pay handsomely for it, and a museum is where it belongs."

"Be very careful, Vansi. The more you take from people, the less power you have over them – and be very afraid when they have nothing left to lose. You will not be a thief, not this day."

"Enough talk!" Vansi was rattled, but defiant.

As he bent down to grab one of the sled's harness shafts, he was surprised by the sight of a currawong landing on it. Vansi waved his arms to frighten it off, but the bird responded with a noisy call as it stood its ground.

"You'll have to try harder than that if you want to rid yourself of Jalwahn the Loud."

Edda spun around to see who had spoken.

"Alex! What are you doing here?"

"A little bird told me you might need some help," Alex replied with a wry smile.

"You have no business here!" spluttered Vansi.

"This is not business, Vansi. This is theft. As always, your greed shrouds the difference."

"Do not lecture me you phoney," Vansi snapped. "I know who you really are, who your grandfather was … and I know the sled should be mine. You owe us."

Edda listened to the exchange in bewilderment.

"What is he saying, Alex? Who *are* you?"

There was a silence, then Vansi spoke, every word, every syllable, dripping with sneering bitterness.

"Tell her, Alex Mansfield. Tell her who you are, not who you say you are. Tell her, just like your father and grandfather, you've spent your whole life hiding your true identity with lies."

"I don't understand. What is going on?" Edda asked.

Vansi pointed an accusing finger at Alex. "Admit that your grandfather was Olaf Lynchford, from the very people who cursed my family."

Alex was more than a little irritated by Vansi's attempt at claiming the high ground.

"Perhaps now, Vansi it's time for *you* to come clean," he said calmly.

"Yes, I've already worked that bit out," Edda said. "He is the grandson of Bani Vansi who I read about in Olaf's diary. He's been following me for days."

"Edda, Vansi's family has hounded our people for what seems an eternity."

"But Alex, what's this about your people being the ones who cursed the Vansi family?"

"His people cursed Vándr Vansi generations ago when he travelled to the coast to buy a boat," Hefna Vansi cut in. "Vándr disappeared on that trip never to be seen again. That curse is now on all the Vansi family ... but I will get our revenge now." As Vansi moved once again to grab hold of the sled, Alex stepped forward and blocked his way.

"Harkon the Loud's curse was not on Vándr Vansi or on your family but on thieves," Alex said.

"Nonsense. It was your secretive Viking clan, your kin, who targeted Vándr and drowned him."

"Not so," said Alex. "He drowned only because he chose to be a thief. The curse that is on you, on your family, is your greed and your vengeance. That is the real curse, one that has corrupted your family from ancient times. We are not set against any person or family. Your family was part-Stórmenska, accepted by us, embraced by us. You know that the idea of us and them is not a part of our culture, not even a part of our language. Our instinct is to respect all."

Vansi laughed. "And look where that got you! Your home by the White Sea was destroyed, Himinnsled was stolen, you have been forced into being refugees hiding in the wilderness, the Christians once jailed and hanged your Seers, and now you have to hide your precious sled at the end of the Earth."

Alex was annoyed. "Yes, the sled had to be hidden far away, but all along it was being shadowed by a Vansi with a craving for revenge and greed. From the time your grandfather, Bani Vansi, arrived here in the mountains over a century ago, he showed his true colours, sneaking around stealing prospectors' gold. I am not surprised at seeing yet another descendant of Vándr Vansi grasping at what is not theirs. Our troubles are not a result of our generosity but your self-seeking *them and us* way of seeing the world."

"You're wrong about my way of thinking," a livid Hefna Vansi said. "It is not *them and us*. It is *them and me*. There is no *us*." Throwing caution to the wind, he continued to speak as if spitting venom. "You don't know the half of it, do you? When Olaf went missing, it was Bani who took over his gold mine." Hefna, pointing in the direction of the resort, continued his tirade. "How do you think I got to own most of the resort over there? Where do you think the money came from? You Lynchfords have always been losers, and with the last of Olaf's possessions in my keeping, I will be a winner again today."

With that, Vansi made an awkward lunge at the sled. Immediately, the ever-vigilant Jalwahn flew at Vansi causing him to fall back onto the snow. Vansi's attempts at getting his bulbous body above his feet proved futile. Each time, as he fell back, he wheezed and scowled, until, eventually, he decided he could try no more. Attempts by Edda and Alex to lend a hand, to get him off the snow, were angrily rebuffed as he flailed his arms and smacked their hands. For Vansi, accepting any assistance from them was a humiliation. He lay helplessly on the snow, muttering curses of revenge that soon rose to a wailing crescendo of self-pity.

Just as he was again beginning to cast himself as a victim, having all but given up on the sled, Vansi heard in the distance a familiar sound. It was the droning hum of snowmobiles, many, many snowmobiles. The frustration of a spoilt child that painted his face turned into a dark, sneering grin.

The clones were coming.

FIFTEEN

ANDVARI'S SCOURGE

Edda's parents and Don had arrived at the ski trailhead at Falls Creek Resort that led to the High Plains.

They set out for the short ski to the Nordic Bowl where they were expecting to meet up with Edda and Finn. With the morning sun shining and a slight breeze, it was the sort of day that brought a crowd out onto the snow. Cross-country skiers were skating and gliding in every direction.

It took some time to realise that the two young ski tourers were not at the agreed meeting place or on any of the nearby ski trails. There would be no reunion just yet. The grown-ups were not too concerned, however; after all, the two were expected sometime during the day and it was still early. Completely unaware of Edda's current plight, they decided not to go out to look for her and Finn on the High Plains. The pair were probably on their way, safe and sound, they thought as they began to return to their agreed rendezvous spot.

Alex and Edda could see something Vansi could not. Still lying as a fatigued heap on the snow, Vansi was not in a position to see the specks emerging on the skyline some distance away – a line of clones standing and scouring the High Plains. They were no longer looking for Edda. The clones, dim-witted and leaderless, were lost.

One clone, turning to scan in the direction of the snow cave, squinted into the glaring white expanse. He took a long, second look at the tiny figures in the distance. Before he had time to alert the others, a skier shot through the middle of the group, took to the air over a cornice and raced down the slope below. The clones looked on with barely passing interest until they realised the skier was their one-time prisoner. On what seemed to be an almost vertical slope and skiing like he had never skied before, Finn was at the very edge of his ability with a laser-like focus on one aim. *No matter what the cost, he must draw the clones away from Edda.*

By the time the soft snow allowed the clones to get back to their snowmobiles, Finn had reached the bottom of the slope and was hurriedly shuffling his way up the next. The clones were in pursuit. For now, Edda and Alex were safe. Leaving what wit they had behind, the clones raced down the precipice in disarray. Those who managed the descent without rolling their machines were thrown from their mounts as they attempted to climb the next steep slope. Finn looked back at the mayhem and was buoyed by the unexpected success of playing the decoy. Feeling safe for a time, he headed in the direction where he, like the squinting clone, had caught sight of Edda.

While Edda and Alex had been watching the whole fiasco play out, Vansi had slithered over the snow to use a length of rope to attach the sled to his snowmobile and dragged his body aboard. The sound of the engine starting set off a scramble to stop the sled from being towed away. There was no need. In a fluster, Vansi had the engine roaring at full throttle. The snowmobile's tracks were wildly churning, getting it bogged down deeper in the thin cover of soft snow. With the engine screaming, and without warning, the snowmobile's tracks had churned through the snow to hit solid ground and violently lurched forward. The rope snapped, and Vansi was thrown back onto the sled. With that, the sled started to move.

Vansi could not believe his luck. He was slipping away on the sled he craved. Edda and Alex watched on helplessly as the sled picked up speed with the shafts folded forward as if being drawn. Vansi turned and beckoned Edda to catch up.

"The ring, I want it! Throw it on the sled," he barked. With no response from Edda, he lay back on the sled and laughed, wallowing in the knowledge that at least the sled was finally his.

Edda, distraught at losing the sled, did not notice Andvaranaut with its wolf head motif start to glow brightly on her finger. The sled turned around, back to the direction of where Edda and Alex were standing. Vansi began to panic at the thought of being delivered back to his two rivals, until the sled took to the air.

"So, it is a magic sled after all. I knew it!" an astonished Hefna Vansi reasoned. "It must be worth so much more money than they let on with their nonsense about an icon of generosity. Generous people! Nonsense. All along they were just trying to hustle me out of the money I should have. They're just as selfish as everyone else I've ever met."

Vansi had the sled to himself, and believing it was worth real money, he revelled in the knowledge he had won the day.

As the sled passed over Edda and Alex's heads, Vansi looked down and laughed scornfully. It abruptly stopped. He was overcome by feeling nauseous, lightheaded and troubled that he was no longer alone on the sled. He looked around to see a large wolf next to him with a prolonged snarl that had the effect of bearing sharp teeth. Vansi glared at its long fangs, knowing their terrible purpose was to tear flesh. He shrieked, then shouted a few words before loudly squealing over and over.

"What is going on?" Edda asked.

"He's shouting something. I think he yelled wolf," Alex said.

They looked again at Vansi, baffled; there was no wolf to be seen.

They watched on as Vansi gradually stood with all the urgency his over-fed frame could muster with the intention of escaping the wolf by leaping off the sled but stopped short. Looking down, he realised he was now too high above the ground. The sled abruptly turned to fly towards the nearby lake in Rocky Valley.

As the sled flew over the lake, Vansi, seeing a gap in the ice, decided the only way to save himself from the wolf was to jump through the gap and into the water. Edda and Alex watched as Vansi leapt off the sled to plunge into the freezing lake below then struggled to pull himself out onto the ice.

There was a time when the lake would freeze as a thick, solid cover extending all the way to the far shore. In more recent times a solid covering of ice had become increasingly rare.

The thin cover of ice surrounding the gap Vansi had jumped into was not capable of supporting his weight. With no quick way of getting out of the freezing water, the winter wilderness was set to claim the last of the Vansi clan.

As he floundered helplessly in the icy water, Vansi shouted in desperate defiance, "I am the spirit of Fafnir the dragon. You will never rid yourself of me! Wherever you go, I am there!" A string of curses was soon rendered to gurgling bubbles.

The clones, a little worse for wear, had reassembled some distance away, but close enough to witness their leader's shouts of anguish from a flying sled before he disappeared into a deathly cold lake. Unaware of the true nature of the sled, or the curse, they could only see a terrifying force was at play. They no longer had a leader and were never going to see the rewards Vansi had promised. As the sled flew directly at them, a moment of hesitation was followed by blind panic. Scurrying to their machines, they scattered like autumn leaves in the wind, harassed along the way by a flying sled and a very loud pesky currawong.

Free of would-be thieves, the sled turned again, passing over the Finder to retreat towards the snow cave. Hitting the cornice at speed, it caused a veil of fine snow to erupt into the air. When it settled, there was no sign of either a snow cave or the sled.

"Alex, is the sled lost again?" Edda asked in dismay.

"It has left us for now and for good reason, but your work may not be over, Edda," Alex replied solemnly. "One day, I hope the sled will be returned to its people. You, the Finder, may be needed yet."

"If so, I guess I will again be guided by Jalwahn."

"I think not. With you as the Finder, and the last of the Vansi family, the last of the people responsible for the theft of Himinnsled at the Mann-fell now gone, Jalwahn's work is done. He may finally be free to join Bodin in the Under-world. What *is* certain is we live in hope of still needing you to fulfil your role as the Finder."

"I don't know why I was chosen to be the Finder, do you?"

"I should," Alex said sheepishly. "I have known you almost from birth. It was no coincidence that I suggested Don should take you along to look for the gold mine. I knew you had all the makings of a Finder even back then."

"Is it because you knew I could keep a secret?"

"More than that, Edda. More than you know, more than I am able to tell you right now."

"The clones have seen the sled, so I guess it is no longer a secret," Edda said.

"I can't imagine many people believing their story," Alex replied.

"Still, word is bound get around."

"I don't think it matters if it does," Alex said. "It will be treated as just another tall story, a mountain myth. These days, there are many concocted stories about people who live by ancient traditions. Stories that degrade the past by picking over events and hollowing out meaning, belittling both our ancestors and their culture. The authentic history of people who live in the natural world seem to be either ignored or raided to make a profit from trite clichéd images like Disney animations or tawdry theme parks."

"Will the sled's lesson of generosity ever be heard?" Edda asked.

"When the rich landscape of real, lived history of a people has been levelled by arrogance and pious criticism, timeless lessons can no longer be seen. When people are beguiled into a self-absorbed, comfortable view of the world, the ground is laid bare for the storm clouds of greed to gather and overshadow us all."

"Do you think that is happening now?"

Alex started to speak, paused, then shrugged his shoulders.

"You'll see."

Edda turned on hearing her name being called. Squinting and scanning into the glaring landscape, she saw a figure skiing towards her across the undulating plains to finally emerged from behind a rise.

"Finn, is that you?"

Rushing towards each other, they found themselves in an embrace that lingered beyond a simple reunion of friends.

"Where have you been? Are you okay?" Edda asked.

"Yeah, all good. Did you find the sled?"

"I'm guessing it will only be found when the time is right."

As they relaxed their embrace, Edda noticed Finn's eyes move to her lips. As he again moved closer with his lips stalking Edda's, she pulled him into the haven of a hug.

Better the angel you know, she thought.

Finn, in that moment, felt awkward and eager to move on.

The pair made their way back to where Alex was waiting.

"We'd better keep moving," Finn said. "The clones are looking for you."

"You don't need to worry about them," Alex replied. "They have scampered away, back to the comfort of the resort, if they can manage to work out the way."

"Did you follow today's riddle?" Finn asked eagerly.

"I don't think there are any more," Edda replied, as she plunged both hands into her backpack.

Retrieving the map, she was surprised to see that there was a new riddle, which she quickly read to herself while Alex and Finn watched on.

'Discovered with the sled! Now Bani's greed
springs ever bold
For safe keeping, I have now buried it deep in the
winter cold
The stalking Bani now craves the sled, I fear what
he may do
Better than gold said he, more bounty for me,
what a coup
Better than gold said I, you know not why, it's
not about you.

He has seen the sled but not where it lays
Smitten with greed he searched for days
Revenge he now seeks in so many ways
Woe is me; for this meeting a price there must be
Woe is me; for this meeting with a deadly Vansi.'

"No!" cried Edda. The shocking insight was like a blow to her head. "It can't be."

"What?" Finn asked. "What's wrong?"

"No one knew what became of Olaf," Edda said sombrely. "He never wrote in his diary, nor was he seen again after he went into the mountains that winter. He is trying to tell us his fate. All along, the riddle's tale of woe was not about us, it was about him! He died protecting the hiding place of the sled. It was the deadly Bani Vansi who did away with Olaf out here in the seclusion of the back-country. It was Bani Vansi who was then free to rob his gold mine."

"Really? What happened while I was away?" asked Finn.

"Never mind. It looks like our quest was just a dead end."

With the newfound knowledge of the last days of Olaf and the theft of his gold by a Vansi, Edda's normal inclination to feel badly about Hefna Vansi's drowning was sorely tested. It was replaced with a feeling of devastation for another. A feeling that was forged by a bond between the Keeper and the Finder. A bond that had stretched to find its mark over a span of a hundred years.

"It's time for us to make our way to the Nordic Bowl and call it quits," Edda said. "We are expected there."

Edda and Alex made a solemn pair as the three set off towards their rendezvous. However, their gloomy mood did not last long. Finn, unaware of the discovery of the sled and the ensuing skirmish over it, was more concerned with entertaining them with his escapades since being kidnapped near the Hill of Trees.

He had never had such an adventure and talked non-stop as the three skied to meet the grown-ups. Absorbed in telling his story, Finn noticed nothing as they skied passed a group of workers winching an upturned snow groomer that had plunged off the side of the mountain.

"We are so glad to see you. We were starting to get worried," Don said as the three arrived at their destination at the Nordic Bowl. "How was the trip, Edda? You must have some stories to tell?"

"No, not really. It was all very straightforward."

Anticipating Edda again standing on his toe to silence him, Finn promptly took a step away.

"Yes, all just as we planned," Finn added.

Alex smiled.

PART 3

FUTURE

*The purpose of looking at the future is
to disturb the present.*

—Gaston Berger

SIXTEEN

HOMECOMING

Edda stepped from the train into the familiar clear heat that summer north of the Great Divide promises.

It had been five years since the discovery and loss of the sled, and, despite several ski tours on the High Plains over those years, Edda had not seen any sign of the cave that comes and goes, or of Jalwahn. That eventful winter had become merely a memory that no longer felt quite real. The sled, Olaf's map and the diary had receded into a past life, one that had been displaced over the years by new phases and pursuits that continued to appear on her horizon. Edda and Finn had remained close, destined to become life-long friends, corresponding regularly, and, on occasion, meeting over coffee where they found themselves in general agreement over the state of the world and where it was heading.

Finn's harboured hopes that their friendship would blossom into something more never materialised. His tendency to display his feelings for Edda by stepping in to guide and protect her found no purpose, only a mild irritation that niggled Edda. Since their quest, Edda was not the same person. Common ground between them was a little more elusive.

Settling into her family home, where Edda intended to spend her summer break from university, mindless routine might well have overtaken the novelty of being reacquainted with her family but for the selection of hefty books that seemed always to accompany her. Sitting alone in her bedroom, the eventual onset of boredom paved a path to idle curiosity. Staring beyond her reflection in the dresser mirror, Edda once again drifted into contemplation. As she embarked on another of her dreamlike journeys, her reflection in the mirror faded bit-by-bit to be displaced by events and images that dwelt along the path of her excursion.

Even though she did not know where her meandering mind would take her, she trusted her own image would reappear in the mirror at a time when, perhaps, she had tarried too long – when exploration had drifted into self-indulgence. When the humility necessary for worthwhile reflection had given way to wallowing in nostalgia.

Edda's vigilance preventing self-interest in her contemplations creating her own comfortable world in the mirror had a purpose. She knew that in the absence of this kind of restraint, her reflections might cross a subtle boundary from a world of useful contemplation to a shallow world that would beguile her into the snug reassurance of an echo. On this occasion, Edda's journey took her to an unknown future. She pondered how as an adult she would find her way in the world, whether she would turn out to be the type of person she wanted to be and would live in the sort of world she would like to inhabit. Despite her self-imposed vigilance, she was ever so subtly drifting away from a world of her lived experience, a real world, towards a gratifying illusion in which she would be who she wanted to be, in a world she would gladly inhabit. An imagined world where self-indulgence loitered. On the perilous cusp of these two worlds, her own image re-emerged to gaze back at her in solemn judgement. An image that then proceeded to repeat the words Alex had once said during Edda's training on his orienteering course, words that explained to her how she could avoid getting lost, how she could best find her way.

"If you persist with a superficial assessment, you will end up making a habit of re-imagining the real world, and those you might blame for its problems, to suit your comfortable opinion. And it is easy to do better than that," he had said.

Her image then pointedly lowered its eyes to the secrets drawer that housed Olaf's diary.

Sliding open the drawer, Edda removed the diary and detachedly began flicking through it. As she turned the pages, however, Edda's uninspired mood changed to shock as she saw her past reappear. Not from recollections of the trip into the mountains with Don or the search for the sled with Finn, but by what in that moment presented itself. There, in front of her eyes, hovering and quivering like a feeding hummingbird, was Olaf's map. Carefully plucking it from mid-air, she slowly unfolded it. She recognised the handwriting on the back of the map immediately. Unexpected and unsought, a new riddle appeared.

> 'The sled cannot rest until it is home
> To find a Keeper the Finder must roam
> Start with the gift when a groom kissed a bride
> Therein lies a course; follow the needle that
> will guide
> Therein lies a course; but courting peril if time
> you bide.'

Edda's thoughts were whirling. "What does this mean for me, for my summer break?" she wondered. "Alex cautioned that I may be needed again."

The longer she sat contemplating the riddle and reciting it to herself, the more she felt it was simply too puzzling to unravel.

Responding to a tentative knock, Alex Mansfield appeared behind a flywire screen door. He looked old and frail, although his red timber cottage remained ageless and his garden, as always, was neat and ordered.

"Oh, it's herself, all grown up. I thought the day would come when you would pay a visit. I have often thought about you, wondering why meeting up again has taken us so long."

"To be truthful," Edda replied, "I put the diary and the map out of the way and out of my mind. Last week was the first time I had opened it for years."

"Come in," said Alex, opening the door wide. "I'll make us a pot of tea. I'm keen to know about what you have been up to."

With five years to catch up on, it was some time before Edda and Alex finished chatting and sipping tea. Only then did Edda hand Alex the map so he could read the new riddle.

As he read, he stroked his generous beard – always an indication that he was deep in thought or at least wanted to give that impression.

"Well," he said finally. "We know that the sled must be found and returned. You somehow must resume your role as a Finder … and soon."

"Yes, Alex, that may be what it says, but what does it mean? Why the urgency and what is the course to follow? I cannot work it out. I thought you might know something."

"I can't imagine what the gift is that the riddle says is the place to start," Alex replied, "It sounds like it's a wedding gift if it came when a groom kissed a bride, but I don't know of any special wedding gift that my grandfather received. All his belongings were left right here in the cottage, with maybe just a few things left in the old gold mine."

"We found some of Olaf's things up there when I went with Don."

"His diary, you mean?"

"That, and a few other things in an old chest."

"Anything interesting?"

"When the chest opened, we removed and kept a small tin box that had Olaf's diary in it, but I memorised what we left behind."

Alex raised a single eyebrow, indicating he wanted Edda to continue.

"Just some old books, a picture of Olaf's mother, pen and ink, and some writing paper, that's it."

"Nothing that might be a wedding gift?"

"Not really. And if there was such a gift, why would it be stuck up in the mine?"

As the pair pondered the mystery, there was a lingering silence, which was broken by Edda.

"Do you know where the chest came from?"

"My grandmother told me Olaf had that chest when he first migrated to Australia. She said it was a parting gift given to him by his mother to store a bulky object he had to transport to Australia, an object that would fit neatly inside the chest."

"A gift, but not a wedding gift. We are still at a dead end." Edda was feeling dejected enough to abandon the idea of being a Finder. It was a role she had only half-heartedly resumed in any case, and she had not received the answers she'd hoped for from Alex.

After a long dismissive exhaling, she got up to go.

After a warm hug followed by promises to keep in touch more often, Alex spoke.

"I'm sorry I could not be more help, Edda. I thought we had a possible lead. I know that after she married Olaf, my grandmother often admired the chest because it was made in a traditional style, especially for his mother."

"Oh, so in the beginning it was *a gift to Olaf's mother*," Edda replied thoughtfully. "Of course! The photo of her in the chest was the clue I missed. When did she marry?"

"That's easy to find out. Olaf researched his family tree when he learnt about his connection with ancient Vikings. Stay put … I'll dig it out."

"So, Olaf's line starts here with Harkon the Loud," Edda said as she studied the lines on the family tree.

"He's Olaf's oldest known ancestor on his mother's side," Alex replied. "Olaf couldn't find anything that goes back any earlier. For much of his life, Harkon was a fugitive from South people, hiding as a lone nomadic herder. I guess not a lot survived besides oral history before he came out of hiding in the wilderness to build a cabin. I have added a little to the family tree, but it's about time I added more."

"You told me you have no descendants. Who is there to add?"

"Do you remember that winter back on the High Plains when you asked why you were chosen to be a Finder?" Alex asked.

"Yes, at the end of the search for Himinnsled, just before we met up with Finn. I remember you said I was chosen for reasons more than you could tell me."

"Well," continued Alex, "Olaf had a twin sister who accompanied him to Australia and started a family here. It's time I added some of her early descendants to the family tree. Like Olaf, she and her family chose to live close to the mountains and the High Plains."

"They would be your cousins. Do I know of any of them, any of her descendants I mean?" Edda asked.

"The true identities of any living descendants of Harkon have been left off the family tree and will remain secret until they have passed on. I will also be added, as Lief's son – Olaf's grandson – when I pass. It is what we have all done to help keep the secret of the sled safe. But I guess the time has come for you to know."

"Time to know what?" Edda asked, puzzled. "Know the name of Olaf's sister and her descendants?"

"Time to know that *you*, Edda, are one of her descendants. Her name was Hedda, and she was your great grandmother on your mother's side. That's why you are a Finder, a role that one day may have to be passed on to your own descendants," Alex said.

"You knew this all along and didn't tell me!"

"I may not have told you, but I prepared you, Edda. Remember the time I devoted to coaching you in mountain craft so you could fulfil the Finder's role."

Edda was silent for a moment or two as she absorbed what Alex had just revealed.

"And Don ... does he know?"

"No. Not Don. Your mother knew of Hedda but little of her background. Don is a dear friend, but there was also a purpose behind the friendship … to encourage him to seek out the lost gold mine and take his granddaughter with him the moment the sled's one hundred years of concealment had ended," Alex explained.

"So, all this time you were waiting for me, waiting for the concealment years to end, waiting to come out of the shadows to involve me," Edda said. "I must admit, I was seriously thinking about ditching the whole idea of being the Finder. I wanted to consign it to the wastebin of history and move on with my life. But I guess that's not really an option now."

"I guess you're right," Alex responded with a private sigh of relief.

With her renewed sense of enthusiasm, Edda immediately threw herself back into the role. Studying the family tree with fresh vigour, she asked, "Who is this *Runa*? Why does her line on the family tree end?"

Alex shrugged. "My father received news from Norway of Runa's birth, but we have heard nothing since. She and the rest of the descendants of Harkon's daughter, Tua, are a mystery since the birth of Runa generations ago."

"So, we know nothing of Runa. She is a dead end," Edda mumbled as she continued to scan the family tree. Her eyes hesitated on an entry that caught her attention.

She smiled to herself.

Alex knew the family tree intimately and was more concerned with deciphering the riddle. Looking again at the back of Olaf's map, he recited it out loud, finishing with:

'Start with the gift when a groom kissed a bride
Therein lies a course; follow the needle that
will guide

Therein lies a course; but courting peril if time you bide.'

"Of course!" he exclaimed. "Hearing it out loud, I realise I missed the clue."

"What clue?"

"The bit I read out where a groom kissed a bride. The clue was hidden. It's not *kissed a* bride, it's *kista* bride!" Alex replied, spelling out the word.

"What is kista?" Edda asked.

Alex smiled, a little pleased with himself that he had detected the clue.

"It is just as well you sought me out, Edda. Kista is a word in our old language. It is a word borrowed from the Old Norse of the seafarers when our two peoples merged."

"Well, what does it mean?"

"That's the thing, Edda. It's the answer to the clue. For us Stórmenska, a kista is a chest. It is the chest up in the mine that is the gift the clue is talking about!"

"Oh, that. I already worked that out."

"What? How could you? You don't speak our ancient tongue."

"Look here in the family tree," Edda said in a matter-of-fact way, devoid of any smugness. "I noticed Olaf's mother was married in 1869."

"So?" Alex quizzed.

"So, 1869 is the year that is painted on the chest. I remember that from a decade ago when I was in the gold mine with Don," Edda continued. "As soon as I saw that wedding date on the family tree, I worked out that the chest must be the gift, the wedding gift, a place where *therein lies a course* that I must follow."

"We agree then," Alex said. "The chest must be your next port of call. Your quest didn't actually come to an end after Hefna tried to steal the sled and it vanished back beneath the snow. It was merely interrupted for a while. Edda the Finder, you are now back in business!"

"Well, I first need to find this needle to guide me," Edda replied. "Let's hope I'm not looking for a needle in a haystack!"

SEVENTEEN

A GOLD COMPASS

Edda set out once again for Olaf's gold mine.

Memories of walking along the same track with Don a decade earlier came flooding back, although an image she remembered – the mystery of only snowgrass growing on the side of some mountain spurs and snow gums growing on the other – was not as she recalled. The snow gums that had once flaunted their vivid smooth bark, a gift from nature Edda would say, were now twisted relics. Dead and leafless, their bleached ghostly forms were a sickening reminder of the Great Divide Wildfires that had recently destroyed much of the alpine environment over two consecutive summers.

(Edda was not to know that this was just the beginning. Later that same summer, one of Australia's worst wildfires would consume scores of national parks and reserves in what would be remembered as Black Saturday. With subsequent wildfires now becoming more regular, these ancient snow gums would have no strategies to recover. They may be lost forever.)

Finding the mine again was fairly straightforward, but Edda's memory was hazy for the task ahead. It took an hour of searching and stumbling through tunnels that followed the small fault lines marked on Olaf's map of the mine sketched on the back of his letter before the chest appeared in the beam of her torch.

"Therein lies a course," Edda whispered as the lid of the chest swung open. Inside, she found the items just as she remembered. She removed the items one by one and placed them on the ground then closed the lid and sat on the chest to examine them. After what seemed an eternity of flicking through books, scrutinising the sheets of writing paper and staring at the faded photo of Olaf's mother, she again had reached a dead end. There was nothing that suggested a course to follow, as the riddle promised.

"Perfect," Edda murmured. "I started with the *gift when a groom kissed a bride* – and zilch, no course to follow." Frustrated, she stood up, tipped the chest on its side and gave it a vigorous shake. Nothing. Edda then noticed that some of the lining on the bottom of the chest had shaken loose. She pushed it aside and her eye caught a glint of gold. "Don *thought* there might be some nuggets of gold in here!"

Eagerly, she pulled the lining away from the base of the chest and shone her torch inside to find it was not a gold nugget that glinted, but an old nineteenth century gold compass. Turning it over in her hand, she could see the initials 'O.L.' on the inside cover, while an inscription on the back read, 'Happy 13th Birthday Olaf. Trusting you will never again lose your bearings when skiing into a forest – 15th March 1889.'

> '**Start with the gift when a groom kissed a bride**
> **Therein lies a course; follow the needle that**
> **will guide**'

It was the needle on the compass that would give her the course to follow, Edda realised. Hastily finding her way back through the tunnels, Edda stepped back through the mine entrance and into bright daylight. She flipped the compass open. The needle spun excitedly as she held it, until, slowing to twitch a few times, it settled. Placing it a distance from her own compass to compare them, Edda saw the needle was clearly pointing west of magnetic north. After looking at the map in the case that she always had with her when venturing into the bush, the thrilling prospect of following the compass needle to the sled here in the mountains was fleeting and rapidly discarded. Following Olaf's compass would quickly take her out of the mountains, away from the High Plains.

Edda was more than a little miffed. "Perfect. Another dead end."

Staving off her disappointment, Edda gathered both compasses and placed them in her backpack before starting the trudge back to the car.

An idea came days later, arriving as a niggle in the night. Jumping out of bed, Edda surveyed a world map she brought up on her computer screen. Holding Olaf's compass in one hand, she noted the bearing shown by the needle. Following its direction, she scrolled and zoomed until the screen revealed the rough-hewn coastline of north-west Norway.

A realisation hit her as she broke the night's silence with a whisper. *"To find a Keeper the Finder must roam."*

Edda realised that she was not just a sled Finder, she first must find a sled Keeper. To follow the compass needle faithfully, she had to roam. In this case, it had to be all the way to Norway.

⁓⁓⁓

On reaching Oslo Central Station, Edda again checked the needle on the gold compass. *'Go west'* it indicated, confirming what it had shown the last time she'd checked, at the airport a mere twenty minutes earlier.

Boarding the early morning train service to Bergen, she retrieved a novel from her backpack and settled into her comfortable window seat. Devouring yet another novel would condense her seven-hour journey by transporting her to a different world that was waiting to be discovered among its pages. It was a useful strategy she often employed to pass the time on long journeys, although on this occasion it would prove to be flawed.

In a short space of time, the train had entered a picturesque valley with glimpses through a forest of a swift-flowing river. Edda was at first distracted by the view, then captivated when the train climbed into rugged mountains blanketed by the first falls of winter snow. After climbing higher, above the tree line, the train commenced its traverse of the desolate expanse that is the Hardangervidda plateau, buried under a deep blanket of snow.

Completely enthralled by what was on display, Edda's eyes did not stray from the landscape – so much so that she barely blinked each time her view was fleetingly obstructed by clouds of snow blasting past her window as the wedge plough on the front of the speeding locomotive exploded through yet another snow drift. While the train barrelled across the plateau at a good clip, Edda had no way of knowing she was crossing the onetime path taken by Harald and Snö-frid when they were on the run from an angry mob over a thousand years earlier.

Edda ate her lunch in the buffet car, but throughout her meal, she remained transfixed by the scenery – now a display of tall waterfalls and deep fjords as the train descended towards the coast and its destination at Bergen.

Returning to her seat, Edda noticed her book still sitting on the small table where she had quietly put it aside. With the journey soon coming to an end, it looked a little forlorn with a bookmark that had not progressed one page since Oslo. Edda returned it to her backpack.

Leaving the train, Edda made her way on foot to the location of her overnight stay, a block back from the Bryggen wharf. Walking along the waterfront, Edda stopped to admire the colourful steep gabled timber buildings that occupied the harbour district. A local woman passing by stopped next to Edda.

"They are beautiful, aren't they, the old buildings?"

"Yes, quite stunning." Edda replied, a little surprised by the woman's decision to stop and chat with a stranger.

"I'm Sissel. I work here at the waterfront."

"Oh, hi. I'm Edda."

"Edda! Like *The Poetic Edda*?

"I haven't heard of that. What is it?"

"It contains Viking mythology written by Icelandic Skalds as far back as the tenth century. What an unusual name. How did you get it?"

"I don't really know. I've never thought about it."

"Well, I'm sure you were given a name like that for a reason. Maybe, in a way, you have come home."

"I live on the other side of the world and know hardly anything about this place."

"Did you at least know that this harbour has been continually active as a trading port since the twelfth century?"

"No, I had no idea," Edda said, realising the interest being shown by Sissel was a combination of her being friendly towards a visitor to her country and deep pride in her small harbour city.

"You know the city has grown from a tiny settlement surrounded by the Seven Mountains a thousand years ago?" Sissel continued.

"I would like to explore this place a lot more, but sadly, I cannot stay," Edda said. "I'm on a bit of a mission, but I should definitely return some day and spend time here."

"Well, safe travels and good luck with whatever your mission is," Sissel responded as she continued on her way.

Edda walked on for a few paces before stopping in front of one particular heritage building. She was taken by how familiar it looked. The window frames and glazing bars were painted white, presenting a vibrant contrast to the walls – layers of timber boards painted in a rich red coat. The building had a remarkable resemblance to the colours of Felaheim, Alex's cottage and his surrounding timber sheds. The sight prompted thoughts of Alex and his part in her role as a Finder.

Feeling visceral excitement return over her quest, with mounting anticipation, Edda took out the gold compass again to look for any movement on the needle. Now that she had reached Norway's west coast, it was pointing almost due north. From estimating the end point of the compass bearing on her computer back in her bedroom, Edda had a suspicion all along the compass might take her to the far North. A coastal ferry from Bergen was the answer, one that went beyond the Arctic Circle and further than any northbound trainline.

She figured that if she kept an eye on the compass once she was on the ferry, she would know when to disembark.

———※·※———

As the ferry steamed north along the coast, Edda passed the Arctic Circle without realising it. There was no guiding sign, no announcement. It would be another two days before she was able to watch the needle slowly turn to the east. The next port was Tromsø, where many of the other passengers were heading to view the northern lights. It was time to disembark.

Edda gathered her things and followed the others off the ferry and back onto dry land.

———※·※———

Transport from Tromsø presented a challenge, as the compass guided Edda away from the most well-travelled roads and in the direction of what appeared to be nowhere of note. On the positive side, as the needle was now moving by the hour, she knew she must be closing in on her destination.

Edda managed to hitch a ride in the right direction with a local deer farmer, and after an hour or so, they arrived at his farm-stay holiday house at the end of a remote snow-covered road. He invited her inside his house and introduced her to his wife and children, who welcomed her warmly and offered a hot drink and food. As she ate and warmed herself by the fire, she checked the compass again. Peering out a window, the needle was pointing steadfastly in a direction where there was no road, just a clearing of trackless snow leading into wilderness. To Edda, it looked like another dead end, a conclusion that was confirmed by the farmer.

"No, nothing much out there," he replied when she asked.

Feeling increasingly desperate, Edda glanced again at Olaf's compass. "But there has to be *something*."

"Young Runa lives in that direction, but we rarely see her at this time of year."

"*Runa*! You said Runa. I must go there, now."

"There will be time for that in the morning. You must stay with us tonight."

"It's too much trouble," Edda protested.

"It's the off-season. We have plenty of room here – and besides, for some time now, we have been hoping for a visitor from the far end of the world."

Edda glanced out of the window again. The sun was low on the horizon and a flurry of snow danced in the gloom. She then looked back at the warmth of the kitchen and the smiling faces of the deer farmer and his family.

"Thank you," she said. "That would be wonderful."

Next morning, after a good night's sleep, Edda prepared to depart. She had warmed to the small family and was overwhelmed by their hospitality, if a little surprised by their interest in her. She thanked them for their generosity when they offered to provide the transport needed for the next leg of her journey and was delighted when she saw what it was when they ventured outside.

There in front of the farmhouse was a large sleigh, and harnessed to it was a magnificent pure white reindeer, which, the deer farmer told her, had mysteriously appeared at the farm the previous day. Just as Edda's hosts had been, it seemed pleased to see her.

"By the way," she said, as she climbed up to settle herself in the sleigh. "Does this place have a name?"

"The area around here is called Lyngsfjord."

Of course it is! Edda thought to herself.

Despite being given instructions, Edda felt a little hesitant about this unfamiliar means of transport. It took some juggling to regularly check the compass needle and at the same time concentrate on staying in control of the powerful beast pulling the sleigh. Her suspicion that she was *not* actually in control prompted a momentary fluster before realisation struck.

She was not needed for either task.

The reindeer was going exactly where it wanted, in a direction that just happened to coincide precisely with the point of the compass needle. Edda was not 'finding her way' at all. She was being delivered.

It took less than an hour for the old wooden cabin to come into view. The reindeer stopped opposite two large timber columns that framed the front door. It opened as Edda stepped onto the snow.

EIGHTEEN

THE FINDER'S KEEPER

Through a window in her cabin, Runa noticed a sleigh pull up outside and excitedly grabbed her outdoor gear as she opened the door.

Edda watched as the young woman, who was both about her own age and her taller-than-average height, hurriedly pulled on a heavy anorak and woollen beanie before stumbling and hopping her way across the veranda as she attempted to put on a pair of unlaced snow boots. Edda was at once taken by the woman's broad, spontaneous smile as she pushed strands of hair off her face and under her beanie.

Wrapping a scarf around her neck as she rushed towards Edda, Runa kissed her on both cheeks before wrapping her in a vice-like embrace.

Strong girl! Edda noted, as she returned a more restrained hug.

"I've been expecting you to arrive here one day," Runa said by way of a greeting. "But never this early in the day."

"I was staying with a deer farmer and his family just an hour or so away."

They paused to look at each other, as unmet comrades want to do. Edda was drawn to Runa's eyes. She noted their shape, perfect almonds, slightly turned up at their outer edge; *a beautiful shape*, Edda thought to herself. *I have never seen eyes of such intense colour.*

A second impulsive hug confirmed the immediate affinity the two felt.

"Is this the feriehus I read about in Olaf's diary?" Edda asked her. "The holiday cabin when he was a child?"

"Yes, it's the same one."

The young women hugged each other again, sharing a mixture of relief and joy. They knew the importance of this meeting. As Runa ushered her into the main room of the cabin, the solid, seasoned timbers, slightly worn, but comfortable-looking furniture and bright fire burning in the hearth gave Edda a cosy, homely feeling. She stopped and stared at the words, 'Heimórr Himinnsledi' painted on a heavy wooden beam.

"It means 'the home of Himinnsled'," Runa explained. "We are hoping the sled will return here one day, to the one-time home of Harkon," she continued, provoking an immediate expectation in Edda that she was nearing the final episode of what had been, for her, a ten-year saga. She was yet to realise that this expectation was born of hope devoid of any certainty.

The two talked all that day and well into the night. Edda described the events in Australia that were sparked by her grandfather taking her on a search for a lost gold mine up to the time she left for Norway. Runa talked of her family's past, including her common ancestry with Bodin, Olaf, and Alex, all descendants of Harkon the Loud.

"Now that I have found you and with the last of the Vansi family gone, it will be safe for me to retrieve the sled and bring it here to its home," Edda said.

Runa shook her head. "There is a problem with that."

"Are there others like the Vansi's we don't know about?" Edda asked.

"There are always people like the Vansi's in the world, but Hefna was the last one who was so obsessed with the sled."

"Is there no Seer here to be a Sled-Keeper?"

"Many are convinced that there is no Seer. They believe Bodin was the last one."

"Bodin told me as much when we spoke in the ice chamber," Edda said.

"Yes, that sounds like something he would say," Runa replied. "He was known for carrying on about being the last Seer. There are a few who know this is not the case. None of our people would believe the truth, so the truth has been kept secret."

"Secret?"

"After Bodin passed to the Underworld, there have been Stórmenska who possess the skills of a Seer, but in a place where no one thought to look."

"Do you mean they are in hiding?"

"Yes, but hiding in a Stórmenska way … hiding in plain sight. It is still believed that Bodin was our last Seer. That is not to say his grandfather's prophecy about a boy-Seer was not true. The sled had to be taken away for safekeeping, but Bodin's claim of being the last Seer here in the north was false. He believed that because he had no children, no male descendant, there could be no legacy of a Seer."

"So Bodin had an unknown son."

"The descendants of Harkon the Loud continue to be Seers. With no apparent Seer after Bodin, it is *women* from the line of Harkon's daughter, Tua, who have emerged as

Seers. My great-grandmother and the first-born woman of each generation since have been Seers."

"Why is this a secret? Why are you hiding this?" asked Edda.

"Timeless traditions serve us well, but they do not change easily," explained Runa. "That is why, like me, both my mother and grandmother were given the name Runa. It's a forgotten Old Norse word that means secret tradition. We have been silent because we knew we would not be accepted. When the sled is returned, when our culture can be reborn, we Runa will take our rightful place."

"Upsetting one tradition to ensure another," Edda mused. "That sounds a little tricky."

"Sometimes things must change if we wish them to remain the same," Runa responded.

"But how do you know that Tua's descendants will become a Seer, that they possess the skills of a Seer?" Edda asked.

"That is also a little tricky. It is usually hereditary, passed on, but it often only becomes clear in their later life that they are a Seer. A good early indication is a child who is always curious and needs to compulsively reflect and contemplate," Runa replied. "That telling trait is usually a good indicator but often dismissed by others as simple daydreaming."

"It is clear to me that I must find the sled as soon as I can and bring it here so you Runa can, as you say, take your rightful place!" Edda assured her.

"Edda, we Runa may reveal ourselves with the return of the sled, but it cannot be returned to the north just now."

"Why not?"

"South people have recently returned to the North with their unstoppable greed, like an infestation of Vansi's," Runa responded. "They have gorged on and almost exhausted their own world. Now they are looking again to the North, this time to harvest timber. We Stórmenska have lived in harmony with the forest so it can sustain all its inhabitants. We have used it wisely – not to feed the gluttony of the South. It is their reckless way of reducing the spirit of the forest's rich cycle of life to the hollow riches of a balance sheet entry that cautions me to not risk having the sled anywhere near their grasp. It must remain where it is."

"Can't you go somewhere else? Far away from the South people?"

"There is nowhere left we can go. South people everywhere have lost the restraint that comes with living as a part of the natural world. They have become so confident that they are separate from it, above it. They are everywhere, and they are so many … so, so many."

"Am I one of them? In a way I'm also from the South," Edda said.

"The South is more a way of thinking than a place. You will find the answer to that question in yourself."

Edda noted Runa's words for a future reflection, a reflection that would uneasily take her back to her verbal stoush with Hefna Vansi below the snow cave – a time when she had waivered to flirt with the prospect of keeping the sled for herself, when she cringed at the realisation that none is immune from the potent allure of greed. But for now, she felt a sense of urgency driven by a single phrase in the last cryptic rhyme. She did not want to be accused of '*courting peril if time you bide.*'

She asked, "If now is not the right time, then when? It cannot stay where it is for much longer."

"But Hefna Vansi and all the other descendants of Vándr the Skulk – the sled-seeking thieves – are gone," Runa said. "It is safe where it is, surely."

"For a little while longer maybe, but it can only be found in a snow cave, when deep snow has covered the High Plains."

"So, when the South people move on, we will be ready for the sled," Runa said. "It is then that you must find Himinnsled. Only then can we Stórmenska return to our old life by the White Sea. It's your calling, Edda. You are the Finder, our only hope. You must be patient."

"The High Plains still have some winters with deep snow but that is changing," Edda said. "More and more we have winters with only occasional snow often mixed with rainfalls.

"Are you sure this is not just impressions you have?" Runa asked.

"From my memories as a young child learning to ski and going on ski tours every winter, I saw, with a few exceptions, winters gradually getting warmer, and the snow line had risen further up the mountains towards the High Plains. One day, maybe soon, there will not be enough snow for the cave to reappear, for Himinnsled to be found."

"Could be just a short-lived change over your young life."

"My parents taught me to ski on Mount Buffalo. That mountain has now been abandoned as a downhill ski resort because of warmer winters. The chalet there once hired out skates for ice skating on a nearby lake, but ice skating was abandoned many generations ago because of warmer winters. The ski club we were members of have a chalet with its own ski runs. Again, those runs have been abandoned except during a rare big snowfall – and even then, they only have limited use for a very short time."

Runa realised that the time when the South people would decide to move on may come too late for Edda to be able to complete the Finder's task – for the snow cave to reappear. She could see her hopes for the future starting to crumble.

"Why could I not see this in the drum?" Runa lamented.

"Maybe your nature spirits don't know what is coming," Edda said.

"Maybe for our nature spirits there is no sled in the future," Runa replied. "In the future, the lesson of the sled may not be told. What then?"

Edda could feel the urgency to get back home bearing down on her like an impending storm – to get there and to be ready for the possibility of a winter with deep snow.

"Over a century ago, when Olaf concealed the sled, he could not have foreseen what would happen to our winters," Edda said.

"True," replied Runa. But she was thinking beyond this. "Our traditions did not begin with the arrival of the Viking ship, or even back when we first settled in our hidden valley by the White Sea," she said in a troubled tone. "We have always cared for the land as we first found it – when the ice gave it up. In return, it supported us for thousands of years.

"Where do you think we are heading to now?" Edda asked.

"Our ancestors, those who were marooned seafarers, once believed that we humans live in abundant Midgard, between the land of ice in the North and the land of fire in the South," Runa replied. "Are we heading to the beginning of the end of days for Midgard, the end of the temperate age? Is this the real reason why the drum cannot show us a vision of the future? Is this Big Warming the beginning of the end-of-days? A time of natural disasters and conflicts our Viking ancestors called Ragnarök? A time when the world is set aflame, where seas will boil and rocks melt? Is this the destiny for us all? What is the South people's greed doing to us all?"

"Sometimes I feel that my world back home is already being set aflame. If we are heading for a calamity, will the Stórmenska survive?" Edda asked.

"I think we could," Runa said. "Our culture is shaped by survival in an isolated harsh environment that keeps us alert to the need to be generous, the need to work together and to steer clear of the greedy lone wolf."

"So, you're convinced your way of life will see you through the possibility of an approaching Ragnarök."

"Well," Runa said on reflection. "If we are headed for such troubled times and the sled cannot be with us as an icon to shore up our beliefs, I'm not as confident we will endure."

Edda silently mulled over Runa's words. She understood her exasperation resulted from her feelings of impotence and the prospect of unfettered greed being tolerated, even celebrated. Edda realised that the insight into her fear of heights was quite different to this dilemma. Her once debilitating fears of what *might* happen were ultimately dismissed as irrational conjured omens in her head that were unlikely to have real-world consequences. Here in this moment, as she contemplated the possibility of the planet's natural world hurtling towards a cliff, she felt a deep primal fear. Runa's eyes, which had the lively sparkle of polished green emeralds when Edda had first looked into them, were now dull and unresponsive. Sitting together in sombre silence, they gazed into the flickering flames of the fire. Edda reached across to gently clasp Runa's hands. She could not think of a comforting word. In response, Runa lifted her head to give Edda a reassuring smile. It was a brave but failed attempt. What met Edda's eyes was the saddest of smiles.

Edda and Runa both slept fitfully that night. Edda would have to leave in the morning, and the thought of parting ways was heart-breaking for both. While they knew they would always be friends, the sort of friends that, on meeting up again, would simply pick up from where they left off, they also understood what was in store if they never had occasion to meet again – for neither to be able to fulfil their role. Reassuring her that Herinn, the white reindeer, would take her safely back to the deer farmer's house for the night before she embarked on the long journey back to Australia, Runa hugged Edda and wished her a safe journey. Just before the sleigh rounded a bend to disappear back into the forest, their eyes met, carrying unspoken hopes for the future. Each simply raised their hand as a parting gesture.

As she went back into the feriehus, Runa felt troubled at the loss of her friend – a soulmate who had come into her life only to depart too soon. Her mood was lifted, however, when a beam of reflected sunlight from the centre of the dining table announced a gift.

The ancient ring, Andvaranaut, had found its way home.

Back at her parents' house, Edda sat alone in her old bedroom. The room was stark with the walls missing the colourful posters of her childhood. The only decoration left was the large, framed print of the Magritte painting, the one enduring image throughout her life, which now more than ever dominated her sanctuary. Edda stared blankly into her mirror. Prophetic thoughts weaved their way through a boundless labyrinth in her mind, taking her on a journey through a myriad of scenarios, all triggered by what Runa had called The Big Warming.

"Is there hope for the future?" she wondered. "I guess as long as a way out of a labyrinth can be imagined, hope is at hand. And where there is hope, there is a prospect of effort."

Note to self: all: How, over more than a millennium, did the Stórmenska manage to avoid getting themselves into such a mess?

Edda's thoughts were jolted to the Magritte print whose reflection was now dominating the mirror in front of her. She sat for some time studying the discordant image. As with all of his Empire of Light images, Magritte had painted the built environment – human imposition in the shape of buildings – as dark, night streetscapes, which in her mind seemed to have gotten darker over the years, and the natural elements, the sky and clouds, painted as daylight.

It reminded her of a saying used by her old friend, Alex. 'If you want to know the future, look to the sky.'

She knew it was his way of working out what the weather might be bringing. For Alex, looking to the sky, the clouds, was looking to the future. Edda, still staring at the print pondered whether it had become too dark for us in our man-made streetscapes, too close on the midnight clock to avoid a tipping point in the atrophy of the natural world. Too late to prevent an unstoppable, runaway chaos.

Edda whispered decisively, "Yes, Monsieur Magritte, after all these years of having you hang on my bedroom wall, I now see what you may be telling me. For us all in our fabricated world, it is getting late for the sky."

From that moment, at the start of every winter when Edda returned to her parents' home to use it as a base for ski touring trips, the Magritte image on the wall would niggle at her about the urgency to again set out across the High Plains in search of the cave that comes and goes. During the four winters since her return from the trip to find Runa, she had scoured the rolling snow plains with no result. Edda had begun to contemplate that the sled was forever lost. The following winter was uncommon, reminiscent of the past. In the mountains, a pattern of north-westerly winds that brought wet snow and sleet was followed by south-westerlies with extensive falls of colder, drier snow. This pattern was repeated again and again until the Australian Alps were draped in white. By August, blizzards blasted through the mountains, to wildly whip spindrift into the air and expose the ice beneath. Persistent, boisterous storms then arrived, carried north from Antarctica on a mission to goad ocean-like swells of fresh snow across the High Plains. During this long winter, deep snow settled in the lee of knolls and ridges, capped by cornices that mimicked ocean waves preparing to break. Nestled below a lonely cornice, a snow cave appeared for one day – and waited. Some distance away, spurred on by the sight of a familiar keyhole shaped entrance to a snow cave, Edda the Finder eagerly approached.

Edda and Runa would meet again.

EPILOGUE

This is where my familiarity with Edda's story comes to an end. As a doting grandmother, Edda purposefully told and retold her story to me many times over several years, when I was about the same age she was when the lost gold mine was found. Some of her narratives over those years left perplexing gaps in the overall story, while others were bothersome in their repetition. To be as faithful as possible in my retelling of her accounts, I have melded together a measured blend of her many yarns about Himinnsled. As a child, I thought they were only that – yarns embroidered for the ears of a young grandchild.

Since that time, the world has changed, and I have come to understand the importance of what Edda was really telling me, and therefore the importance of retelling her story to my own grandchildren while I'm still about.

Now, beyond the dawn of the twenty-second century, it has been over thirty years since I undertook the task of clearing out Edda's house as part of managing her deceased estate. At that time, while rummaging through a disused, cobweb-festooned shed in her backyard, buried under cardboard boxes of bric-a-brac, I glimpsed an old painted chest.

Once I'd uncovered it, I stood and stared as the chest unlocked itself with a loud creak and clunk and slowly yawned open. Inside, I found neat piles of letters from Finn confined in bundles by rubber bands, a small, well-used spi-ral-bound notebook filled with 'Notes to Self' and an oilskin pouch containing a diary. Folded inside the diary's tattered black cover was a map. I turned it over curiously.

On the back, I watched as a verse wrote itself across the blank page in wet ink. As I read it, in that moment, I was reassured that Edda's story is still one of hope.

The ending of which is yours.

> *'The sky is braking, nature is quaking; who will heed?*
> *Words are spoken, endeavours are token; who will lead?*
> *Still, South people with each thought and deed*
> *Contrive one more need as a homage to greed.*
>
> *Warnings of the Warming are growing old*
> *Yet the truth of its cause is still to be told*
> *Self-indulgence when ushered by greed*
> *Has denied fellowship and selfless deed.*
>
> *The remedy to a looming future we don't want to see*
> *It's the spirit of Himinnsled foiling greed and vanity*
> *Rescued from the snow, it awaits in our common humanity*
> *Himinnsled is no fable; the future is not what it used to be*
> *Himinnsled is no fable; the future of its spirit is our delivery.'*

ABOUT THE AUTHOR

Leon Kildea has worked as a senior secondary teacher, High School Principal, and in education administration. More recently, he was a Founding Director of a company that is passionate about improving the standard of education and support for students and young adults. He lives in Wangaratta, Victoria, with his wife. He has spent much of his available free time traversing remote wilderness areas on skis in the Australian Alps, Norway and North America, as well as a skipper on numerous voyages sailing around the coast of Australia, the Southern Ocean, the South-West Pacific and the Mediterranean Sea. Other outdoor activities Leon has pursued include rock climbing, mountaineering and orienteering – providing lived experience to inform the adventures of this novel's protagonists. Leon is enthusiastic about furthering a better understanding of the environment, the future of the planet and their related social issues. He was responsible for the development and writing of the Victorian Certificate of Education course in Outdoor Education for Year 11 and 12 students, as well as a companion publication for teachers on how to structure and implement the course in the classroom and the outdoor environment.

In this coming-of-age story, Leon uses his background in teaching young adults, and his experience in ocean and mountain wilderness, to explore the protagonist's dilemmas in finding out the kind of person she wants to be and the sort of world she wants to inhabit.

A new voice in young adult literature, this is Leon's first fiction novel.